VINCENT MCKAY

HAPPY TRAILS PILGRIM

Copyright © 2015 by Vincent McKay

Printed and bound in Canada by Globe Printers Ltd.

ISBN 978-0-9865096-1-2

To contact the author:
Telephone: 1-888-949-1877
Office: 1-306-586-2522
Cell: 1-306-515-1117

Published by:
Frontier Book Company
Box 810
Lumsden, SK, Canada
S0G 3C0
Telephone Toll-Free: 1-888-949-1877

About the author:
The author was born on the Saskatchewan plains somewhere between a lake and a sand hill.

Sources:
Kansas City Central Library
Office of the Provincial Secretary - Protocol Office
Regina Central Library – Reference Desk
Maria Anne McKay -the author's grandmother who was niece by marriage to Chief Piapot

How to purchase this book – www.ChiefPiapot.net

This novel is based on certain sourced facts and is self-published by the author, Vincent McKay.

Distributor:
Frontier Book Company
Box 810
Lumsden, Saskatchewan, Canada
S0G 3C0
Telephone Toll-Free: 1-888-949-1877

Dedication

A special dedication to my Assiniboine Grandmother who was born near Wood Mountain and was a niece to Chief Piapot by marriage. I could not visit her house without hearing a story about the exploits of Chief Piapot.

Shout outs

Jon

Andrea

Jessica

Shane

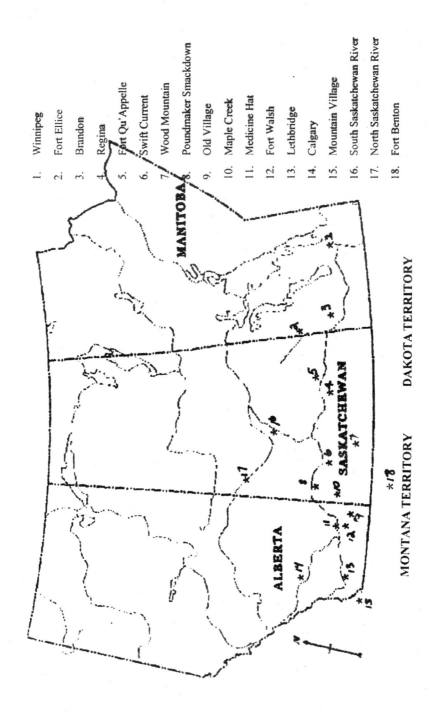

1. Winnipeg
2. Fort Ellice
3. Brandon
4. Regina
5. Fort Qu'Appelle
6. Swift Current
7. Wood Mountain
8. Poundmaker Smackdown
9. Old Village
10. Maple Creek
11. Medicine Hat
12. Fort Walsh
13. Lethbridge
14. Calgary
15. Mountain Village
16. South Saskatchewan River
17. North Saskatchewan River
18. Fort Benton

MANITOBA

SASKATCHEWAN

ALBERTA

MONTANA TERRITORY   DAKOTA TERRITORY

N

Contents

Chapter One

Meet Chief Raincloud

"It is just business, that is what you whites say."

"So what makes you think I am interested in an ambush?" McAllister asked.

"I know you like money."

"Do you think I like money enough to kill the people with whom I do business?"

"It has been said that you would be interested?"

"You know, for an Indian, you speak English very well. Where did you learn your English?"

"Here and there. Mostly at the forts."

"What is your name?"

"Hawk."

"Would you mind telling me who told you I would be interested?"

"They speak about you in a white settlement called Cut Bank. It is said that you lend money but make deals people cannot meet and you have your own Sheriff who takes Deputies to claim the land when they do not pay. Your Sheriff and Deputies have killed several ranchers. You have a daughter that married a rancher and moved southeast just to get away from you."

"Now see here! My family is none of your business! You mention my family once more and I will order these men to kill you! Do you understand?"

"I understand."

The very well educated Mr. McAllister lowered his voice and said to Hawk "Four of my Deputies could very easily follow them and get my money back if that were my intention."

"If your Deputies follow them, they will be slaughtered."

The two Deputies and McAllister laughed loudly.

"You stay where you are while I discuss this with my Deputies."

The three walked a short distance and discussed the situation.

One of the Deputies spoke. "We can send five killers from the ranch. They will have no trouble killing five Indians that drive wagons and we can kill this son of a bitch right now."

"Yes, you are probably right but I am a man who likes the odds. A good gambler never gambles. If they are as heavily armed as that Dillon I cut the deal with, an ambush might be the way to go. It would be fast and neat. Besides, our do good employees at the bank would know about the killings and take it back to Fort Benton. We do not need any Territorial Marshall nosing around."

"Dillon was a white or a half breed," a Deputy stated. "These days you just never know. Hawk over there sounds like he was educated in the east."

"Yeah! He sounds like some kind of big mouth lawyer or something!"

"Take it easy Sam! You are forgetting that a lawyer is what I was before I came here."

"Sorry Boss. This rotten Indian has me upset."

"Then we will kill him after he gives you the information" the other Deputy stated.

"No! I think not. If there is anything I hate, it is a bloody informer. They are the dregs of society but if the information is correct, we can use him again before we kill him. It is worth a few dollars to find out!"

"Dregs?"

"Never mind."

The three returned to speak with Hawk. "Now tell me, my good man, how much money would you be asking for your information?"

"Fifty dollars."

"Fifty dollars! These men here work for two months for that kind of money!"

"Fifty dollars" Hawk replied.

"Let me put a bullet in his head Boss!"

Hawk slowly unbuttoned his coat and said to Sam, "You could try."

The two Deputies moved apart as they got ready to draw.

McAllister stepped forward. "Now just hold on here!" He turned to Hawk and said to him, "I will give you fifty dollars but your information had better be correct. If it is incorrect, I will hunt you down and kill you, your family and anyone else that is with you. Do you understand?"

"The information will be correct."

McAllister reached into his pocket and removed a large billfold of money. He took out two twenties and a ten. He said to Hawk, "Now what is the information?"

"I will need the money first and I will need silver dollars."

"Jesus Christ man! Is there anything else!?"

McAllister, clearly agitated, ordered his Deputies to walk over to the Bank and bring back fifty silver dollars. The two Deputies left swearing and threatening as they walked.

"Why do you need silver dollars?

"Anything more than a dollar is too much money. The white man thinks a silver dollar is about all an Indian is worth."

McAllister looked even more agitated because he did not know how to answer.

In a few minutes, the Deputies returned with the silver dollars and McAllister handed the bag to Hawk.

"Well then?"

Hawk spoke. "The four wagons will come at you from the northeast and the four riders will ride northeast when they leave. When they reach the Snake River, they will turn west. All you have to do is ride straight north and set up your ambush by the Snake River. They will ride straight into the ambush."

"Exemplary! I mean very good!"

McAllister was clearly pleased.

"Now tell me. You obviously know these people quite well so why does it not concern you that they will all be killed?"

"It is just business. That is what you whites say."

"Somehow, I feel as though I am paying you to take care of your business. Is there anything else?" McAllister said.

"Maybe one thing. There will be a rider with them that you will not see. He will watch from a high place. He is Sioux and rides a solid black. Him you must try to kill first for he can kill you all. The wagons are on their way and will be here the day after tomorrow."

"What is the name of the Sioux?" McAllister asked.

"Death!"

Hawk turned his horse and rode north. As they watched Hawk ride north, McAllister and his two Deputies laughed at his warning about the Sioux he called Death.

"We will give that Sioux son of a bitch death all right!" Sam exclaimed.

"I do not think this guy is lying. No! Try to kill the Sioux first. Ride out to the ranch and pick four of the best. I will send Luke to let you know when the deal is completed. Tell the riders they will each get a twenty five dollar bonus for their trouble."

Sam left for the ranch and McAllister sent Luke to watch for the wagons.

Before noon of the second day, Luke returned to the ranch and informed McAllister that the wagons would arrive within hours. McAllister sent him to the ranch with the news.

Shortly after noon, McAllister and his drivers watched the four wagons approach with the lumber. They were leading four fine riding horses tied behind each wagon. The wagons stopped a short distance from McAllister. He watched the four riders as they bridled and saddled their horses. McAllister looked for the solid black but could not see a fifth rider.

"Jesus, they are as heavily armed as that Dillon guy!" McAllister exclaimed.

A young rider of mixed blood approached McAllister. "My name is Jonathan. You must be Mr. McAllister?"

"That is correct."

"Everything is on the wagons as agreed. I would prefer one thousand dollars in paper and two hundred in coin. I will need the money before your drivers take the wagons."

"Of course."

McAllister sent a driver to the bank for the money.

"I would like to take a quick look at the loads," McAllister stated.

"Of course," Jonathan replied.

McAllister took the reply as mockery which made him wonder just who the hell these people were. McAllister was satisfied with the loads and the driver returned with the money.

McAllister handed Jonathan the money and ordered his drivers to the wagons.

"What happened to Mr. Dillon?" McAllister asked.

"He had business to attend to at our settlement. He said to say Hello."

"Yes, well say Hello to him and you fullas have a nice ride home."

"Thank you, we will."

Raincloud watched his four young riders approach. He ordered them ahead as he rode behind. The shadows were still short when they reached the Snake River and turned west.

Late in the afternoon, Raincloud looked west and saw magpies take flight a distance ahead of his riders. He saw a doe and two fawns dash from the thicket. He sensed danger and rode with speed.

Raincloud heard the rifle shots and galloped his horse up the slope tying his reins as he rode. When he reached the flats, he saw three of his four riders down with five shooters riding hard toward them.

As Raincloud neared, he saw Thomas aim and bring down a shooter before their bullets knocked him from his horse.

With rifle in one hand and ammunition belt in the other hand, Raincloud slid from his horse and ran toward a narrow ravine. The four shooters rode hard towards him. Just before the ravine, Raincloud went to a knee. He opened fire, knocking two riders from the saddle and hitting a third one high up in the shoulder. As he rose and leaped for cover, a bullet high in the leg spun Raincloud around knocking him into the ravine. He limped with his good leg downhill through small brush and waited.

In just seconds, the two shooters appeared at the top of the ravine. Raincloud let go a blast blowing a hole into the side of a shooter's head. As he dropped to the ground, his horse reared blocking Raincloud's vision. The other shooter turned his horse and rode away with great speed. Raincloud made it to the top of the ravine just in time to see the shooter mount his horse after picking up the saddle bag of money. There was only time for one more shot. When he was near the slope, Raincloud went to a knee and fired. The shooter dropped the money bag and hung on to the saddle horn with both hands. Just before the slope, he fell from his horse and did not get up.

Raincloud looked at the bodies on the ground and he could now feel pain from the leg wound. He climbed on a horse and rode from one body to another putting bullets into the heads of the four shooters. As he approached the shooter near the slope, he could see his hand reaching out, grabbing grass as he tried to crawl forward. Raincloud shot his right hand so he could not reach for his holstered pistol. The shooter made only a faint cry. There was not much life remaining. He was shot through the back and high up on the left shoulder. Raincloud slid from his horse and removed the holstered pistol. There was no rifle in sight.

He rolled the shooter over with his boot and said to him, "I am Raincloud."

"You .... are .... Deathcloud," he replied in a whisper.

"Yes, I have killed many times. I am going to ask you a question. If you do not answer I will take this knife and remove both your eyes from your head."

"No! No!" "Do .... not take .... my eyes!"

"We rode northeast from the McAllister settlement and turned west where the river snakes to the mountains. How did you know we would take this trail?"

"McAllister told us. He promised to pay us twenty-five dollars each to bring back your horses and the twelve hundred dollars he paid you for the teams and wood."

"Who told McAllister?"

"We asked him but …. but …. but he said …. It was none of our …. of our business."

"And it is none of your business how I let you die. There is a wind and the wolves will smell the blood. They will eat you alive if you do not die before they come."

"Do …. Do not leave …. me."

"You still have one good hand. I will leave you this bullet and your pistol."

Raincloud mounted his horse and did not look back. As he rode towards his riders, he heard a shot and it amused him.

Back near the fourth camp, Dalton scanned the plains with his glass eye but could not see Raincloud on the trail below.

Dalton turned his horse and said to William, "They are late. We will ride the trail east. You ride back to the camp and bring ten warriors and two medicine men with strong medicine."

William rode west and Dalton took his seven riders East along the Snake River.

Raincloud knew he had to stop the blood. He rode over to the horse with medicine and removed the saddle, bridle and medicine bag. Taking his razor sharp knife, Raincloud cut away the steel ring that held the leather straps that secured the saddle. He cut away the cloth from the wound where the bullet entered and exited high up on his leg. Most of the blood came from one wound. He cleaned both wounds with the almost pure alcohol that was in the medicine bag and then secured the ring around the wound. In great pain, Raincloud stretched out on the grass with his head on the saddle and waited.

After two hours of hard riding, Dalton reached a high place where you could see for miles along the east trail. He took his glasses and scanned the trail.

"I see them! Jesus! It looks like a massacre! There are bodies everywhere! Let's ride!"

In less than an hour, the Dalton party arrived on the battle field. Raincloud raised his rifle and waved it back and forth. Dalton rode quickly to Raincloud and slid from his horse.

"Do not try to get up. We will look at your wound and speak later."

Dalton got to his feet and ordered two of his warriors, who knew something of wounds, to take care of Raincloud.

A warrior stopped his horse and reported to Dalton that everyone on the ground was dead.

Dalton said to the warrior, "Gather all the horses and put their saddles and bridles in a pile and let them graze. When you are done with the horses, place our warriors together on the grass and place the others a short distance away from them."

The warrior left immediately and Dalton went to speak with Raincloud who was a little groggy from the medicine given to him from the small bag.

Dalton asked Benjamin, "How is he?"

"The wound is infected but the blood is almost stopped thanks to the steel ring he put around the bullet hole. There is no bullet to remove so we cleaned the wound and put on new cloth. When the medicine comes, he will sleep and we can kill the redness."

"Will he be able to ride?"

"No! He will need two or three days rest."

Dalton walked to Raincloud and took a knee beside him. "Can you tell me what happened?"

"Yes. I was riding a little behind to …."

Dalton placed a hand on Raincloud's shoulder and said to him, "Take it easy. We are in no hurry."

Raincloud went on to explain exactly what happened. "So you killed the remaining four?"

"I had to. There was no one else."

Dalton laughed and said to Raincloud "You saved the nation twelve hundred dollars but look at this saddle. You cut the ring out and ruined a good cinch!"

They hit each other on the shoulder and had a good laugh. Dalton had a bond with Raincloud as Chief Piapot did with Three Killer.

"You must stay here for a few days. Our people will move you across the Snake to the ravine just in case."

Raincloud nodded.

A rider reported to Dalton, "Chief Piapot sent two riders by train to Lethbridge. They have brought the news that you have been appointed Chief of Chiefs to replace Three Killer and everyone is very pleased. Chief Piapot asks that you travel to the Fort."

"I want you and three others to take our four warriors to the fourth camp. Send a rider ahead to have Beth attend. She will know who lies in the ground and who lies in the trees. I will ride North to Lethbridge and to the Fort. Tell Joseph to ………."

"Joseph left for Calgary to visit" the young rider interrupted.

"I put Wandering Buffalo in charge. Tell him to spread the warriors along the trails."

"I will take him the message, Chief Dalton."

Dalton turned to Raincloud. "I feel sorry for Beth. She put Chief Three Killer, who was like a father, in the trees less than two months ago and now she must bury her grandchild.

Raincloud looked at the ground and did not speak.

"Do not blame yourself for any of this. What about me? I was supposed to ride with you but I stayed behind to study maps. If it were not for you, we would be out twelve hundred dollars, not to mention the saddles, bridles and four horses we gained."

"They are good looking horses but two of them have grease or something on their legs" Raincloud offered.

"It is nothing. They walked in the mud where the ranchers grease their wagon wheels. Have the young fullas cut the long hair and rub off the grease with alcohol."

"What about the money?" Raincloud asked.

"I will take two hundred dollars in paper and two hundred dollars in coins. Chief Piapot likes coins."

"Here! The five sons of bitches had about forty dollars in coins. Take these too!"

"It will be enough for me to buy white man clothing, get a haircut and pay for the train. Send two riders south to talk with Chief Charlo. Have them ask him if his people saw a rider cross his hunting grounds in the last few days. Have the riders report to me and no one else. I will be back in ten days. I will need permission to take the nation to war."

Dalton took his horse north across the Snake and rode hard for Lethbridge.

Chapter Two

Piapot Sends for Dalton

"This peace is killing me, Dalton."

It was a hot day in June as the train steamed across the plains rattling and shaking on the small rails. Dalton looked out the window with a certain amount of sadness. He looked for buffalo even though he knew they were gone. It was the first time he saw the plains since the train robbery and the white man was everywhere plowing and fencing the land.

Toward noon of the second day, the westbound pulled into the Regina Station. Dalton entered the station and looked around for his sons. It was not long before Samuel, Michael and Mary spotted him and ran to his side. Dalton almost cried for he had not seen them for six years.

After hugs all around, they left the station where Pete Gopher waited with his wagon. "I have a buggy but we thought it might bring attention to us" Pete stated.

"You are right. The wagon is just fine."

Dalton gave Pete a shoulder hug and the four headed north to the Reserve.

When they reached the Reserve, there was a large crowd gathered to greet Dalton. Some knew him and some just heard about him.

Pete Gopher stopped the wagon in front of the Great Hall and Dalton stepped down. There were handshakes and shoulder hugs all around.

Chief Piapot stepped forward and spoke. "Let the Nation meet Chief Dalton, the new Chief of Chiefs who will replace the great Chief Three Killer in the mountains. It has been a long journey for Chief Dalton and he will now go into the Great Hall for food and rest. The weather is fair and the feast we have prepared will be held outside on the planks starting at six by the white man's clock."

Piapot, the Elders and Dalton proceeded to the Great Hall where the women were busy putting food on a long table. There were potatoes, Piapot beets, rabbit, fish and the white man's chicken that did not fly.

Dalton was seated beside Piapot and Pete Gopher sat beside an elder at the other end.

"It will be a light meal before 'The Feast'" Piapot said.

"There is plenty here and I am hungry" Dalton replied.

The food was passed around and Dalton ate his share.

"This chicken tastes like the meat we cook outside" Dalton stated.

"Yes! Our men are starting to cook but so far only meat. Look towards the kitchen, Chief Dalton. Do you see that large chimney that was not there before?" An elder asked.

"Yes."

"In the lodge that bends steel, the men have made the round pieces pounded into a frame. The smoke from the wood passes through the meat as it goes up the large chimney. Just like outside."

"This I will take back to the mountains! I will even start cooking."

Dalton turned to Piapot, "This chicken has something on it that gives it a sweet taste along with the smell of the wood. It is very good."

"Yes. The French women mix a sauce with honey and some kind of pepper. The men rub it on the chicken with a spoon."

"Jesus! What would we do without our French women?"

There was laughter from the table as the French women praised Dalton.

When the meal was over, Dalton said he would like to rest for a little while and meet again at three or so. They all agreed and Dalton left the Great Hall.

While Dalton was gone, the crowd spoke among themselves. They spoke mainly about Raincloud and wanted to change his name to "Four Killer."

Piapot and the Elders discussed the massacre and agreed that McAllister would have to wait. They decided that is was time to move the younger people out of the mountains as soon as possible. They spoke of a man to the west called Landsdown who could help get the papers for those who wished to be of mixed blood and those who would go to Reserves.

Early in the afternoon, Dalton returned to the Great Hall. He was shaved and his black shoulder length hair shone from the steam. He wore a white shirt tied at the neck, a black striped suit and vest with black polished boots. The women told him how handsome he looked as he walked to the long table and took a chair across from Piapot.

"I suppose you have heard about the ambush" Dalton stated.

"Yes. We have been read the telegram you sent from Lethbridge. Also, David has told us about the money you gave him. It is much money and we are pleased to get it" Piapot replied.

Dalton nodded.

An Elder spoke. "We want you to know that you deserve to be 'Chief of Chiefs.' You have done much for our Nation and it is not only our wish but you are also the choice of Three Killer. He would not have put you in charge when he was dying if he did not want you to be Chief of Chiefs."

Several other elders spoke well of Dalton who lowered his head for like Piapot, he was not a man of praise.

"I am anxious to slaughter the McAllister people!" Dalton exclaimed.

Several of the elders looked to Dalton and then to Piapot.

"We will go to the Warriors Room" Piapot said to Dalton.

The two took their mugs of wine and proceeded to the Warriors Room and sat at a small table.

Piapot spoke. "In the last few days, I have heard much about McAllister. It is always a pleasure to kill this kind of man for he is not only our enemy but an enemy to all people."

Dalton nodded and said to Piapot "How does it feel to be here in the valley and at peace with the Blackfoot?"

"This peace is killing me, Dalton."

There was belly laughter from both as they banged their mugs on the table and took more wine.

Piapot continued, "There is talk in the camps about a young Cree from the valley who stole horses in the Yankee Territories. He made the mistake of selling them to a rancher who did not have a closed mouth. The police heard of it and had the young Cree returned to the Yankee Territory for trial. The Yankees hung him.

When you go after McAllister, do not leave any tracks. There is no more of our land left for them to steal so the Canadians and Yankees now sit cross legged."

Dalton nodded.

"I will tell you now why the Elders wanted us to speak.

The Police gather more information each day about our people.

They try to find out who is of mixed blood and who is not. They do not want Indians written as mixed blood with the same rights as whites. The elders agree that our people who wish to be written as Indians should come to the Reserve soon."

"What about those who wish to be written as Mixed Blood?"

"There is a man in Calgary who speaks from both sides of his mouth!"

Dalton smiled, for this was the way Piapot described a lawyer.

"His arm reaches across the plains to Ottawa and his wealth grows with each day. I think you should speak with him for he sounds like the kind of man who can do anything if you have money. Is there money in the mountains, Dalton?"

"Yes! We have not even spent all the money from the train robbery. We have made much money from potatoes, wood and gold and it costs us very little to live. Even some of those we have put into business have paid us for their stores and land."

"Good! Now before you take the nation to war, you must put our people back on the plains. How many are there?"

"About one thousand. I will remain in the mountains along with the dog warriors. No one under fifty-five years will be allowed to remain. Our women can no longer give us children so we will die off in the greatness of the mountains."

"Even before McAllister and putting our people on the plains, you must find this person the white man calls informer. If he does not get what he is looking for, he will go to the police and tell them everything.

"Maybe he did it just for money," Dalton added.

"He could not get enough money to do what he did. It is something else."

"What else could it be?" Dalton asked.

"They do it out of jealousy and sometimes out of fear. This person did it out of jealousy. There is something he wants but does not know how to get it. Walk softly Dalton, if you corner him, he will run to the police for protection. Do not let him know you are coming."

Dalton nodded.

"Could it be one of the Flatheads?" Dalton asked.

"No, the Flatheads hate traitors. You should see what they do to them."

Dalton looked away for he knew Piapot was right. The Flatheads had no way of knowing the day or the trail that was taken.

"So it is in the nation?"

"Yes" Piapot replied.

Dalton looked away again for he did not want to hear the truth.

"When you find him, no matter who he is, kill him and anyone else who knew and said nothing."

Dalton nodded.

"I would like Vincent, one of the stonebreakers and Thunderchild to come to the mountains."

"Vincent and Louise are in Winnipeg."

"I bet Vincent wishes he was in the mountains."

"No, Vincent likes Winnipeg. His father-in-law made him part of the business and he has learned even more about numbers. Louise would like to live in the mountains for she says the grandparents spend too much time with the children. Already, the oldest one of the two is in a special school. The grandparents have a religion much like us for they speak directly to the Creator."

"Maybe we have found some rich Indians!"

They both had a good laugh and threw back some more wine.

"Vincent and his family call themselves Lugar" Piapot added.

"Lugar?" Dalton said with a laugh.

"Yes. The grandparents thought it would be better for the children.

Piapot continued. "David you cannot have for he is a man of the cross. Benjamin Stonebreaker is in Winnipeg and he will go with Vincent to the mountains."

"What about Thunderchild?"

Piapot lowered his head for a brief moment and spoke to Dalton.

"I will tell you now about our Reserve. At the start, many of our young people tried to find work with the whites but they did not want anything to do with us. Now and then the whites will hire some to pick stones or potatoes. Our young riders are the best on the plains but they could not even get work herding cattle.

At another Reserve, our people farmed some land. In the fall, they loaded up a wagon with wheat but were turned away at the elevator by the police. A white farmer who lives nearby followed the wagon to the Reserve and bought the grain for the same price as the elevator would have paid.

Just when you feel like giving up on the white man, something like this happens. The farming stopped and most of the machines were picked up by the white settlers. The rest of the machines just turned to rust.

There is very little money coming into our Reserve. We live on rations and what we grow. With nothing to do, our young people get into trouble. Mostly because they steal to buy the white man's goods. They are put in jails and numbered as trouble makers.

From time to time, the mixed bloods come to visit and will bring us bags of flour and sugar. Sometimes they even bring a few cattle. In the evening some go to the shacks with tobacco and whiskey. They have become much liked by our young women.

Many of our young people have built shacks. They do not wish to live near the Great Hall where we can see them. With the few dollars they earn and steal, they buy the white man's whiskey and even the things that are used to brush on houses. The white man no longer sell them whiskey with poison but they have found how to make it even worse.

These shacks they call houses have poles piled one on one. They do not even use mud and straw in between to keep out the wind. There is no floor and they sit on wooden boxes around a small stove in the center where they heat the poison mixture. When it boils, each one puts a skin over their head to cover the pot as they take turns breathing the steam. The women are as bad as the men.

They do this as often as they can and it makes them too drunk to work and too stupid to steal."

This was a serious moment for Piapot but Dalton was amused by his words.

"I will take you to Thunderchild now but before we leave, I will tell you that the McAllister massacre will be the last massacre for our Nation."

Dalton nodded and they both left the Warriors Room to join the Elders in the Great Hall.

After a short visit with the Elders, Dalton, Piapot and two of the younger men left for the shacks. When they arrived at the Thunderchild shack, the two young men opened the door and Dalton and Piapot stepped inside. Dalton looked around and it was just as Piapot described. Two women and four men sat around a small fire. They saw Dalton and looked away. The smell of stench and poison filled the room. Dalton stepped forward and the six lowered their heads.

"I am looking for a brave warrior who sat on the right side of Chief Piapot at the Poundmaker meeting."

No one spoke and not one of them raised their heads.

Dalton continued. "His name is Thunderchild and is the grandson of the great Cree Chief who was called Chief Thunderchild."

Thunderchild slowly raised his head and tried to focus on Dalton. His eyes closed and opened. He tried to speak but only slobbering noise came from his mouth.

Dalton watched as Thunderchild put a foot out to stand, only to fall backwards on the dirt floor. Thunderchild began to crawl towards Dalton. When he made it to where Dalton stood, he reached up with both hands, hung on and clutched the jacket sleeve of Dalton. He made it to his feet and looked straight into Dalton's eyes. Dalton put a hand on his shoulder to steady him as he spoke.

"I .... I am so ashamed .... Chief Dalton."

"It is not your fault. I want you to come to the mountains for there is some work we must do."

Thunderchild nodded.

Piapot said to the two young men. "Take him to the Warriors Room. Put him in the water and find him clean clothes. Make sure he gets something to eat and let him sleep."

The young men nodded and took Thunderchild away.

"I cannot believe it has come to this in less than ten years" Dalton said.

"Yes. A short time ago we were hunters and warriors. Look at us now!"

Piapot and Dalton spoke as they walked to the Great Hall to meet with the Elders.

"Do not worry about Thunderchild. He will be ready by the time Vincent and Benjamin arrive from the east."

It was late in the afternoon and already many gathered near the planks waiting for the feast.

"It would be good if you spoke to the Nation before the feast" Piapot said.

"Yes. But only a few words."

"That would be good too!"

This brought much laughter. Piapot had a way of amusing the people he liked.

As they neared the Great Hall, many followed Piapot and Dalton. Dalton was a legend to the young for they had never seen him before. Some wanted to shake his hand like the white man but Dalton touched their arms with his forearm. As he walked, the people had words of great praise for Dalton and they congratulated him for being chosen as Chief of Chiefs in the mountains.

Once inside the Great Hall, the Elders wanted to know if Dalton agreed with what would be done first in the mountains. Dalton agreed with the order in which things came first and assured the Elders everything would be done very soon.

An Elder sitting across from Dalton spoke. "I notice you do not shake hands which is a white man custom."

"I am not a white man. I am Assiniboine."

There was a loud noise in the Great Hall as everyone cheered Dalton. The Elders at the big table banged their wooden mugs and yelled for more wine.

Outside, the crowd increased as people came from the nearby Reserves to hear Dalton speak to the Nation.

Riders moved throughout the crowd to make sure there were no Police or strangers among them.

At six o'clock, Dalton emerged from the Great Hall and was greeted by hundreds. Piapot stood on his right and Pete Gopher stood to his left.

Dalton stepped forward and spoke. "I do not have to tell you that four of our young warriors were ambushed by five killers sent by a man by the name of McAllister. We believe they were betrayed by a Flathead informer."

The crowd yelled for revenge as Piapot smiled and looked down at the planks.

"Let me tell you this! McAllister and the informer will die for what they did. If we do not find the informer, the Flatheads will. They are hated in the Flathead Nation."

The crowd cheered and many shouted. "We will ride with you, Chief Dalton!"

Dalton raised his hand and waited a few minutes for the crowd to settle down.

"When I was a young man, over thirty years ago, I came to this valley from the Yankee Territory. I met a Sioux warrior and we hunted buffalo together. Maybe you have heard of him, his name is Chief Raincloud."

The drums pounded and the crowd roared. They shouted, "Four Killer! Four Killer!"

"We asked Chief Piapot if we could ride with him. He allowed us to ride with him and he made us a part of the Assiniboine Nation.

We fought the Blackfoot, the Sioux, Wolfhunters, whiskey traders and we worked each day to feed our people. I have been to the shacks and I can tell you that the white man thinks he has succeeded in creating a new kind of vegetable but I will tell you that the Assiniboine Nation will rise and nothing can stop it!"

There was a roar from the crowd.

"This is a time of darkness but if you put the Creator at the head of your table, you will find daylight. Each day our Nation has thanked the Creator for the sun, for the rain and for all things. This is what savages do and this is what we will continue to do.

Over the years I have had the honor of sitting cross legged with many great Chiefs. I have learned that a great Chief hunts first and eats last. This is what Chief Piapot has done for our Nation and I consider it an honor and a privilege to do the same."

There was a roar from the crowd and the drums pounded as Dalton stepped down from the planks to walk among the people. Piapot and Peter Gopher walked with him.

The feast began and continued after dark. Small fires were everywhere as groups gathered to talk and sing. Piapot, Dalton and Pete Gopher walked to a very large tent. There were planks on the floor covered with buffalo skins and a small stove off to one side to heat pails of water for the basin. There were candles everywhere and a small fire pit in the center.

Dalton was impressed with the tent and told Piapot and Pete Gopher of his appreciation.

"We know you do not sleep inside and you have come a great distance to visit" Pete Gopher stated.

"Yes, and I have not had a good day like this in a long time."

Pete Gopher lit a small fire. The three sat cross legged and discussed the Reserve situation. Young women soon arrived with wine, mugs and a bottle filled with a clear liquid that looked like water.

"Why do we need water? We have water here" Dalton asked.

"This is something like whiskey only stronger I am told. I will add a little to the wine" Piapot answered.

Piapot poured three mugs of wine with a little white whiskey and the women gave Dalton and Pete Gopher each a mug.

Dalton took a sip of the wine and his eyes lit up.

"I taste the chokecherry but there is something else" Dalton said.

"Yes, the women added the juice from the red berry that the white man calls raspberry."

"Of course! My God this is good wine!" Dalton exclaimed.

Piapot told one of the women that they would need some food. At first they hesitated to leave for they were pleased to be in the company of three important men. Four of the five girls left and soon returned with platters of cooked meat, berries, and soft biscuits.

After a few drinks, Dalton got up to go outside. He took a few steps and could feel the drinks.

"We had better slow down or we will soon be in the shacks!" Dalton exclaimed.

This brought laughter from everyone.

"We do not need any more of this white whiskey" Piapot stated.

The talk turned to the buffalo.

"How many have you got in the mountains?" Pete Gopher asked.

"There are about three hundred. We take the old bulls and cows for our use so the herd is young and strong. They are divided into three locations and we move the bulls from location to location.

Dalton could see that Pete Gopher was deep in thought.

"Tell us what you are thinking about Pete" Dalton said.

"Every time I ride on the plains I feel a great sadness when I do not see the buffalo. Without the buffalo it is as though we never existed. It is as though we never made our own way and it is all a dream."

"That is how I felt when I came on the train and that is why I no longer ride on the plains. I have not ridden on the plains for six years."

After a few hours, everyone left except for one fine maiden who was told to stay and help Dalton clean up.

Early the next morning, Pete Gopher and Michael along with Samuel and Mary arrived in the wagon. Dalton gave Mary a hug and said to Michael, "I guess you know that the Nation needs you to go south into the Yankee Territory."

"Yes. I will leave with Thunderchild and the rest."

Late in the afternoon, Dalton and Pete Gopher arrived at the station and Dalton boarded the train for Calgary.

It was the summer of 1889 and Dalton, "Chief of Chiefs" was fifty-six years old.

Chapter Three

Meet Sarah Walker

*"She would spread her legs for a rock pile if she thought
there was a dollar in it!"*

In the forenoon of the next day, Wildfire waited on the
planks and greeted Dalton as he stepped down from the
train.

"It has been a few years, Chief Dalton."

"Yes. It is good to see you again, Wildfire."

Wildfire brought a horse for Dalton and they talked as
they rode. Wildfire explained that his family was located
on a road coming from the south near the settlement
on the Bow River. He told Dalton how a lawyer in the
settlement got his name changed to James Wilde.

"How did you meet this lawyer?" Dalton asked.

"Sarah took us to him."

"You mean Sarah, the daughter of Anne and Big Man Walking?"

"Yes. The lawyer changed her name to Sarah Louise Walker. They are more or less friends."

"Sarah is not yet twenty."

"She is now! Landsdown made her twenty-two years old."

The two had a good laugh.

"This lawyer, what is his first name?" Dalton asked.

"John."

"Sarah was practically raised with a gun in her hand. I used to watch her on the range. She had great speed and accuracy. Does she still know how to hold a gun?"

"Oh yes! Sarah and a couple of cowboys ride out and shoot behind our lodge."

"How did she meet Landsdown?"

"Landsdown defended her."

"What did she do?"

"She killed a cowboy at the back of a saloon."

"Jesus!" Dalton exclaimed.

"The cowboy owed her money and he refused to pay. I guess he threatened her by raising his pistol over her head telling her he would crack her skull open if she did not shut up. That was a mistake. I guess Sarah reached into her bag and blew a hole through the bag and the head of the cowboy."

"Jesus!" Dalton exclaimed.

"Anyhow, I guess Landsdown had done some business with her so when she was arrested, he got her out of jail and later got her off on the white man's law of self-defense. The trial lasted only minutes."

"Were there any witnesses?"

"No. Sarah looks like an angel and that is usually the only witness she needs."

Now you are telling me that the cowboy she killed owed her money and she did some business with Landsdown. Is she a whore?"

"Yes."

"My God! This we have not heard in the mountains. Anne would want to die."

"I know. Sooner or later though, it will come out for she is making enemies."

"What kind of a man is this Landsdown?" Dalton asked.

"He seems fair. He owns the land and lodge where we live and do business. Each month we pay him so much money on a mortag or mortec."

"Mortgage" Dalton offered.

"Yes, a mortgage. Cathy keeps track and we will soon have it paid. The money we were given when we came to the settlement left us with not a lot to borrow and business is good. Landsdown rides out with Sarah now and then to shoot. He seems comfortable with the mixed bloods and brings presents for us when he comes."

"I will want to meet Landsdown. Can Sarah arrange a meeting?"

"Yes. She is coming out to shoot at two o'clock and wants to speak with you about her brother. She wants to be the one to kill the Flathead informer when he is found."

The two reached the lodge before noon and took their horses to the barn for feed and water. Cathy stepped out on the planks with her two year old and greeted Dalton. As they entered the lodge, the business part was filled with all the goods a rancher would need such as bridles, saddle blankets, saddles and clothes of all kinds. Dalton was impressed and told them so.

"Where do you get all these goods?" Dalton asked.

"Landsdown sent a supplier to speak with us and many of the items here are made by the Blackfoot. The cattlemen especially like the long fur coats and chaps for winter" Wildfire replied.

After taking a good look around, Dalton was taken to the rather spacious living quarters. Wildfire and Dalton continued talking while Cathy put the food out. Dalton played with Timothy until dinner was ready and the three continued talking as they sat around the table. The conversation once more centered around Sarah which seemed to anger Cathy.

"She went from a slut to a whore! She would spread her legs for a rock pile if she thought there was a dollar in it!" Cathy exclaimed.

"Well, like they say up and down the Missouri, the only difference between a whore and a slut is one gets paid and the other one doesn't."

Wildfire laughed as Cathy gave him a mean look.

"You approve, Chief Dalton?"

"Well Cathy, she is twenty-two now and there is nothing I can do or say to stop her" Dalton replied.

"That bloody Landsdown made her twenty-two. She is only nineteen."

"I will talk to her. I understand Joseph came up to visit" Dalton stated.

"Yes. He left for the mountains when he heard about the massacre. He was anxious to help out with McAllister.

He bought a few things and gave us ten dollars before he left" Cathy explained.

"I guess he must have sold a little gold to the nation before he left the mountains. Wandering Buffalo watches the money like a hawk after a weasel" Dalton added.

They both had a good laugh.

"How far is it to the target range?"

"Just a few minutes, I will take you there."

After thanking Cathy for the meal, Dalton cleaned up, shaved and put on a new shirt. He gave Cathy five dollars for Timothy and left with Wildfire to meet Sarah.

On the way, Dalton asked if Two Horns was still with George Bull. Wildfire explained that George Bull, Two Horns and the rest lived just a few miles southwest of Calgary and they made a living stealing, buying and selling horses.

Wildfire spoke of how good it was that Joseph took Cathy for his own daughter when Victoria brought her to the mountains.

Dalton told Wildfire he would ride to Calgary with Sarah and wanted to know where he would leave the horse. Wildfire told him to leave the horse at the livery.

Shots could be heard as they rode to the edge of the slope overlooking the range. Sarah, unaware of their presence, reloaded and continued shooting at the target. Dalton dismounted and drew his rifle. He fired several shots at a target blowing away the bulls eye.

Sarah turned quickly and pointed her pistol at Dalton.

"Do not kill me! I only came to practice!"

"Chief Dalton!" Sarah exclaimed.

Dalton walked down the slope and gave Sarah a hug leaving her feet dangling.

Wildfire waved at them as he turned and headed back to the lodge.

"That was good shooting, Chief Dalton."

"I notice you like to get off a lot of shots in a big hurry. You should save a couple in the chamber just in case someone shows up that you were not expecting."

They both had a good laugh.

"I have been gone six days. I went to the Fort to visit Chief Piapot."

"I know. He made you "Chief of Chiefs" and I am happy for you. My brother is dead and I want to ride with you into Yankee Territory when we slaughter McCallister."

"First, there is something I must do. I think you know a lawyer by the name of Landsdown?"

"You mean John Landsdown? Of course I know him. He has helped me out a few times."

Dalton smiled and said nothing.

"I think you have been talking to Cathy. I have been with several men but I also have a job working at the hotel now and then. I say hello and goodbye to rich men and pour the odd drink. I made the mistake of spending a little time with a shit healed cowboy and I suppose you have heard about that."

Dalton nodded.

"If a rich business man treats me like a lady and wants to give me a few dollars for spending a little time, I will take the money."

"I just hope your mother never finds out. She has enough grief what with Benjamin being killed."

"That bloody Cathy! I hear she was quite a slut in her day. She has a problem and I can tell you what it is!"

"I know what it is."

"What is it?" Cathy asked.

"She is jealous of you."

"How did you know that?"

"A wise old chief told me."

Sarah wanted to change the targets before they left and Dalton watched her as she walked on the short grass. She was tall and moved like a beautiful young fox. Her blonde and red hair shone in the sun. The top of her blouse was unbuttoned and showed a well-tanned skin. The color of her skin was not dark and not white but golden and glistened with the sweat.

"My God! She is beautiful" Dalton whispered to himself.

As they rode along the trail, Dalton said he did not want to stay at a hotel and Sarah told him of a fancy boarding house she would take him to. Dalton also wanted to buy new cloth and Sarah told him where to go.

When they reached Calgary, Sarah watched the horses while Dalton bought a new suit of clothing. Dalton soon returned and Sarah rode with him to the bank where Dalton took out five thousand dollars and put the money in his saddle bags.

Sarah pointed to the boarding house and she agreed to bring Landsdown there at three o'clock.

"Remember, my name is Joseph Dillon."

"I will remember."

Dalton registered and went to clean up and change into his new clothes.

Just before three o'clock, Sarah arrived with Landsdown. She introduced Dalton as Joseph Dillon and after a hand shake, Dalton took them to a small meeting room.

"We could have met at my office, Mr. Dillon."

"I prefer our meeting to be as private as possible."

"Fine, now what did you have in mind?"

Dalton paused and said to Landsdown, "What I have to tell you concerns a nation of Indians and it has been a big decision for me to talk with you."

"I am a lawyer here on business and nothing that is said at this meeting will be repeated by me."

Landsdown had a presence about him that Dalton liked. He was well dressed and not fat like most rich people. His mustache and "to the point" attitude reminded Dalton of Superintendent Walsh.

"I will need white man names and adoption papers for about five hundred to seven hundred of my people. I will need you to do for them what you did for Sarah and the Wildes."

"Your people? You are as white as me."

"Yes. I may be as white as you but in my heart I am Assiniboine."

"So am I" Sarah added.

Landsdown looked at Sarah and then Dalton. He smiled and nodded his head.

"This is a lot of people and a lot of work" Landsdown stated.

"Are you able to do this and how much will it cost?" Dalton asked.

"Of course I can do this. It is not unusual now for people to want Canadian identification. Most hunters, trappers and traders did not have a need for identification. So far as the money is concerned, it will cost you twenty dollars per application. Do you have that kind of money?"

"I guess you are talking about ten to fifteen thousand dollars."

"Correct."

"I do not see that kind of money as a problem."

Landsdown looked at Sarah as though he was wanting some kind of confirmation.

Sarah smiled and said nothing.

Dalton continued, "I understand you are involved in real estate and building."

"Very much so" Landsdown replied.

"I can supply you with box cars full of cedar pre-cut lumber. We have four by fours, eight by eight's, twelve by twelves and very much sheathing. The lumber is only seven years old at the most."

"Seven years old makes it only better. I will take as much as you can supply."

"What about cut stone?"

Landsdown put both hands on the table and leaned towards Dalton.

"You mean cut stone ready to place one on top of the other?!"

"Yes, that is exactly what I mean."

"My God man! I will take it all!"

Dalton lowered his head and smiled. Landsdown reminded him of a little kid receiving a gift.

"I will not bargain with you on your price for the paperwork if you give me a fair price for the lumber and stones."

"I will give you a fair price! I guarantee it!"

"The other thing I will want is the purchase of land for those who wish to farm or ranch. Do you perform this kind of work?"

"Absolutely! I have two people in my office who do nothing but perform real estate transactions."

"And what will this cost?"

"With real estate, I work on a percentage and because there is travelling involved, the fee will be ten percent of the total transaction plus disbursements."

"Disbursements?"

"Yes, these are small items we must pay out to complete the transaction. It does not amount to that much."

"What information will you need from me?"

"I only need the name of the purchaser and the location of the land. How much land do you wish to purchase for each applicant?"

"The land will be purchased in sections divided into one quarter per person."

"That is a good idea. That way, there will be families close by who know each other" Landsdown stated.

"Yes!" Dalton replied.

"Now that we are getting down to it, I might give you a little advice" Landsdown continued. "There will be many adoptions and my suggestion is that one of the parents should go to their reserve in order to keep the connection alive.

In other words, when the children become of age, it will be easier for them to obtain reserve status if they choose to go in this direction."

"It sounds good to me!" Sarah stated.

Dalton and Landsdown simultaneously looked at Sarah and then at one another.

"Yes, it makes good sense to me as well" Dalton said.

"Also, the land should be purchased as close to the reserve as possible so the children and parents can visit back and forth without difficulty" Sarah added.

Once again, Dalton and Landsdown looked at Sarah and then at each other.

Landsdown extended his hand towards Sarah and said to Dalton, "This young lady is going to be somebody in this world."

"I think you are right! We will purchase the land as Sarah suggested" Dalton agreed.

Sarah just sat at the end of the table looking good and smiling.

"What about you, Mr. Dillon? I can start your paperwork immediately."

"I took a train to Winnipeg a couple of years ago and got registered as the son of a white trapper and an Assiniboine mother."

"Good! Now I do not wish to throw cold water on this marvelous meeting but I will need a retainer to get things started."

"You mean like a deposit?"

"Yes."

"How much will you need?"

"If you give me a two thousand dollar retainer, I will deliver the registration and adoption papers to you before noon tomorrow.

Dalton placed his saddle bags on the table, counted out two thousand dollars and gave it to Landsdown.

"Jesus! How much money have you got in those saddle bags?!"

The three had a good laugh.

"Sarah! I have some people from the east coming to the hotel for dinner tonight. Will you be available to decorate the room with your presence?"

"What time?"

"Around 6 o'clock."

"I will be there"

Landsdown shook hands with Dalton, gave him a receipt for his money and left the meeting room.

Chapter Four

The Horse Hunt

"I will find the horse."

Before noon the next day, Landsdown arrived at the boarding house where Dalton and Sarah were enjoying a late breakfast.

"Thanks again for coming last night Sarah. Those bankers think you should move to Toronto."

"Who knows! Toronto sounds good!"

Landsdown went over the paperwork with Dalton and gave him samples of how they should be filled out.

They also discussed the lumber and stone business in detail. Landsdown gave Dalton the name of a contractor just outside Lethbridge who would stock the product for shipment. Landsdown once again assured Dalton of a fair price.

"Now just as soon as the contractor sends me a telegram describing the product, I will credit your account for pending legal work. I will send a telegram back to my contractor outlining payment for each load by way of a credit to your account. You can use the telegram as a receipt."

"That sounds fair to me" Dalton stated.

"Who knows, when the smoke clears, maybe I will owe you money" Landsdown added.

After Landsdown left, Dalton and Sarah talked about her involvement in the McAllister massacre. Sarah was to travel with Michael into Yankee Territory to gather information.

"I want to know where he keeps the money" Dalton said.

"I think I will be able to get that information for you. How much is the nation going to pay me?"

Dalton looked at her with narrowed eyes.

"Do not get excited, Chief Dalton. I was making a joke."

"You know Sarah, when you left the mountains for Calgary, there was much disappointment but now that I have got to know you a little better than I wanted to, I think you made the right move.

Now speaking of money, I think the nation does owe you money. The reason everyone else got money was because they were older and had a plan. What would you use the money for?"

"I would like to buy a nice big house like this and rent rooms to wealthy businessmen."

"When this McAllister thing is over, I will make sure you get some money to get started. I will see you again when you arrive with the boys from the east."

It was almost train time as Dalton said goodbye to Sarah and walked to the station.

When Dalton arrived at the Lethbridge station, the first thing he did was to send a telegram to Vincent: 'Pick up everyone including Sarah: Horses will be waiting at the Lethbridge livery: Go to the Strong Eagle Ranch I will meet you there.'

After leaving the telegraph office, Dalton walked across the street to the livery for his horse.

"Gordon will bring you five horses with saddles and bridles probably in two or three days from now. Can you store the riding gear and board the horses in your corral?"

"Yes! Absolutely!"

"Good."

Dalton gave the owner twenty dollars and rode out to the Strong Eagle Ranch.

Strong Eagle and his family watched as Dalton rode up the slope towards the house. They greeted him on the planks and they went inside. Strong Eagle, who was now Gordon Strong, left with the kids to take Dalton's horse to the barn for feed and water.

When they returned to the house, food was on the table and they talked as they ate. Gordon suggested that the informer could have been in the nation but Dalton disagreed and blamed the Flatheads. Gordon agreed to sell him five horses.

The conversation turned to McAllister.

"I hope I get a shot at him" Gordon said.

"Sorry Gordon. Chief Piapot does not want any young fathers going into the Yankee Territory."

"Do you think you have enough fire power?" Gordon asked.

"Yes. Once we get a handle on him, the dog warriors will take care of it."

Heather looked at Dalton and said to him in a somewhat relieved voice, "Thank God for Chief Piapot!"

"I will sleep in the barn tonight and leave for the village early in the morning."

Dalton thanked Heather for the meal, gave her five dollars each for the kids and gave Gordon three hundred dollars for five horses and gear. He also gave Heather one hundred dollars to buy food for the company from the east and the wagon drivers.

The next day, Dalton arrived at the village before noon and was greeted by hundreds who had a hundred questions.

"I want all the Chiefs and assistants to meet me in the warriors' room" Dalton stated.

Within an hour, they all gathered in the warriors' room. Dalton explained that all the buildings would be taken down one by one in order to pay for the final move to the plains.

There was a great deal of sadness but they all understood that sooner or later the white man would find the village and no one would have a choice of where they would go.

When the meeting was over, Dalton asked Wandering Buffalo and Raincloud to join him in the small pool.

As they soaked in the pool, Dalton asked Wandering Buffalo if the money he gave him added up after expenses.

"You gave me five hundred dollars and a few coins. I am surprised you could travel for nine days and put out the money you did for less than five hundred dollars."

"The next time send me, I will show you how to spend the money!" Raincloud shouted.

They were still laughing when the two riders sent to the Flathead nation approached the pool.

"You asked us to report directly to you Chief Dalton" one of the young riders said.

"Go ahead. Did the Flatheads see anything?"

"Yes. One day before the massacre, two of their hunters saw a rider from a distance riding northwest towards the village. They said it was a man but could not make him out because he rode in the shadows."

"What about the horse?" Wandering Buffalo asked.

"Yes. They said the horse was not black and had no white except for white on the head. They said the horse did not have white on the legs or they would have seen it. Also, there were brief flashes of sunlight that came from the side of the horse where a rifle would be placed."

"Is that it?" Dalton asked.

"Yes. Chief Charlo wants us to send the informer to him when he is caught."

"We just might do that" Dalton replied.

"Has anyone asked you about this report?" Raincloud asked.

"Yes. A few."

"I want you to make a list of those who asked and give it to Chief Wandering Buffalo" Dalton ordered.

"We will begin the list immediately, Chief Dalton."

"Did you tell anyone what the Flatheads saw?"

"Yes. We told them the Flatheads saw nothing."

The three smiled and before they left Dalton told the two riders not to mention anything about the report.

"We did not get much" Dalton said.

"We got enough" Wandering Buffalo stated.

Raincloud and Dalton looked at Wandering Buffalo and Dalton asked him to continue.

"The horse was a solid brown with a white star. We will now look for this horse."

"We can also eliminate the women and those under twenty-two years. It may lead to women and others but right now we are looking for a grown man with big ideas" Dalton stated.

"Big ideas?" Raincloud asked.

"Yes. Chief Piapot says it is a man who is jealous and wants something big. Chief Piapot does not think the traitor would inform for a few dollars. I think it has something to do with nation money and position."

Wandering Buffalo and Raincloud nodded.

"Speaking of money, within a few thousand, how much money does the nation have?" Dalton asked.

Wandering Buffalo answered, "In Winnipeg, the Zugars and the Stonebreakers have twenty thousand deposited in banks. In Calgary and Lethbridge, Beth has twelve thousand deposited. In Calgary and Lethbridge, you have twenty-two thousand deposited. With the money you returned, the nation has eight thousand."

"How much is that?" Dalton asked.

"Sixty-two thousand dollars within a thousand or two."

"I want you and your assistants to tell me how much money will be needed to put everyone on the plains or on their reserves" Dalton stated.

"I will have this information in just a few days."

"I already know how much the paperwork will cost. Put down fifteen thousand."

Wandering Buffalo nodded.

"Raincloud, I want you to track down this horse. Do not let anyone know what you are doing."

Raincloud nodded.

When they got out of the pool, Dalton left to visit with his wife and on the way, he ran into Joseph.

"Well Joseph, I think we'll be tearing down some buildings." Dalton said.

"Why?" Joseph asked.

"The village needs some money to put our people on the planes." Dalton answered.

"What would you like me to do?" Joseph asked.

"How about training horses for the wagons?"

"Okay. I will start tomorrow."

Dalton said goodbye and proceeded to his tent.

After a short rest and supper, Dalton and his wife walked from lodge to lodge visiting with the parents of the four young warriors who were killed in the ambush.

They especially spent more time with Wandering Buffalo and Beth who not only lost a son but also her friend Chief Three Killer who was put in the trees just days before.

Early the next morning, Dalton divided up the work parties who would begin tearing down the buildings. The Great Hall and the pool would be torn down last. Joseph was put in charge of training horses for the wagons. Raincloud and Victoria were put in charge of the warriors who would travel into the Yankee Territory. Beth and several assistants were put in charge of the paperwork.

Dalton told Victoria that she would take her orders from Raincloud.

"I gave you Victoria so you would have time to look for the horse. Find the horse and you find the rider."

"I will find the horse" Raincloud stated.

Raincloud gave Victoria her orders and rode to each camp looking for the brown horse with a white face.

On the second day, Dalton gave Raincloud the two riders who spoke with the Flatheads. Raincloud sent them in different directions to observe every horse that grazed. Raincloud continued to ride throughout the camps.

Towards evening, Dalton was taken by the young riders to a high place where Raincloud was waiting.

Raincloud reported that fourteen horses matched the description. Six of them were not trained to the saddle and three of them never left the village.

"So that leaves five horses" Dalton concluded.

"Yes" Raincloud stated.

"Do you know who owns these horses?"

"Yes."

"Were any of them on the list of people who asked questions?"

"No" Raincloud answered.

"Have Victoria tell everyone who has not already done so to bring their rifles to the forge for scraping and painting. Maybe we can eliminate a couple more."

"Good idea" Raincloud said.

A young boy from the village approached Dalton and told him that Strong Eagle sent his son with a message.

They all left for the village and as they walked the boy asked Dalton if he could keep his name on the papers.

"What is your name?"

"Moose."

They all had a good laugh. Dalton gave the boy a shoulder hug and told him to ask Chief Beth.

When they reached the village, they went into the Great Hall and Dalton read the message.

"It looks like our friends will arrive tomorrow morning" Dalton stated.

Dalton told Raincloud he would leave in the morning ahead of the five wagons that were ready. "I want seven armed dog warriors, five on the wagon and two outriders."

"Yes. And I will tell Victoria now about the rifles. I will know how many suspects we have to watch by the time you get back."

"Make sure you watch the five we have already!"

"Like a hawk!"

Dalton went to where Joseph was sitting. He told Joseph to be ready to go in the morning and each wagon would lead a team so they would not have to stop and rest.

Joseph nodded.

Dalton left the Great Hall.

In the morning, Beth gave Dalton two hundred applications and the approximate location where the land would be purchased. She also gave him an estimate of what the five loads were worth.

Dalton and Young Bill walked to the barn where their horses were waiting and they watched as the teams were being hooked up. He told the drivers to meet him at the Strong Eagle Ranch when they were done with the contractor.

Dalton and Bill turned their horses north and rode hard for Lethbridge. It was twelve days since the massacre and Dalton had the informer on his mind.

He remembered several elders telling him about informers and how the police allow them to commit crimes so it is easier for them to gather information. The police will even put them in jail beside you to get information.

"Yes. They are scum. I will find this son of a bitch." Dalton said to himself.

Chapter Five

The Informer

"We are not looking for a Flathead. The traitor is in the nation."

Just before noon, Dalton and Bill stopped at a high place overlooking Lethbridge.

"Tell your mother I will be along soon and the teams will arrive before six o'clock. Say Hello to Sarah and the boys."

Bill left for home and Dalton rode towards Lethbridge.

After taking out one hundred dollars from his account, Dalton left for the telegraph office and got a message off to Landsdown. The message advised Landsdown about the five wagon loads of timber and a rider by the name of Vincent who would deliver a package to him before noon of the next day.

Late in the afternoon, Dalton rode out to visit with the Landsdown contractor who was located on a railroad spur. Lumber was piled everywhere.

Dalton introduced himself and was taken to the contractor.

"Well Mr. Dillon, you sure do not believe in wasting any time! Your teams just left for more lumber."

"Time is money they tell me" Dalton answered.

Dalton liked the contractor right away and was asked to stay for supper. Dalton told him he had to catch up with the wagons but thanked him for the invitation.

"So what do you think those five loads are worth?"

"Well, it is damn good timber and I have valued it at one thousand seven hundred dollars" the contractor replied.

Dalton looked at the estimate Beth gave him and nodded his head.

"I think we can do business" Dalton stated.

"Mr. Landsdown mentioned stones."

"Yes. We will soon have wagons of stones for you when we are done with the lumber. The wagons will be arriving here every day for at least fifteen days."

"Yes, and each day I will send a telegram to Landsdown describing the loads and their value. Starting tomorrow, I will give one of your drivers a Landsdown telegram as a receipt for the amount of each load credited to your account."

"That is exactly what I will need!"

The two spent a little time visiting before Dalton rode out for the Gordon Strong Ranch and within an hour, Dalton caught up with the wagons.

"Be careful with those barrels of wine. There is going to be a celebration tonight."

The drivers whooped and hollered as Dalton rode for the ranch.

When Dalton arrived, the riders from the east were on the planks. Dalton had not seen Benjamin and Vincent for six years. Thunderchild looked like the old warrior he was and Dalton greeted them all with a great deal of enthusiasm. Vincent gave Dalton the money from the east.

"Where is Sarah?" Dalton asked.

At the mention of her name, the young riders went on and on about her beauty.

"She is in the house helping with the food" Gordon said.

The wagons soon arrived and everyone left to help take care of the teams and put them in the corral.

The barrels of wine were placed on the planks and they all filled up their mugs. The seven drivers ate first while the rest remained on the planks drinking wine and eating soft biscuits.

Dalton told Vincent he was to remain at the ranch until all the deliveries of lumber and stones were finished. Each time a package arrives, he would deliver it to Landsdown.

"Also, I want you to keep a record of these loads and credits" Dalton stated.

"I understand" Vincent continued, "I brought a book to record the transactions. Keeping track of what is coming in and going out is what I do."

"Transactions?"

"Dealings" Vincent replied.

"I am going to clear out my accounts in the morning. You will take two thousand dollars to Landsdown and tell him I do not want any delays."

Vincent nodded.

After they all ate their fill, everyone left for the barn and were joined by the families Gordon had working for him. Drums, guitars and violins sounded as the men took turns dancing with the women. Sarah fit right in and was having a good time dancing with the men.

Late in the evening, the party shut down. The families left for their homes and Sarah left for the ranch house with Heather and her two daughters. The rest of the men visited for a little while before bedding down for the night.

Dalton spoke with Gordon and told him Vincent would pay him each day for meals.

"I want you to charge enough so you can get Heather and the kids something nice" Dalton stated.

Gordon nodded and left for the house.

The wagons left early in the morning and Dalton met with Sarah and the four riders.

"We are not looking for a Flathead. The traitor is in the nation" Dalton said.

The five looked at each other with disbelief.

"I think we are getting close. We will find him soon."

Dalton ordered Michael, Benjamin, and Sarah to remain at the ranch and help out. Thunderchild would ride to the village.

"I will ride to town with Vincent and when he returns he will have a sum of money. If you need anything, just ask. You cannot ride south until the informer is found."

Vincent and Dalton left for town and after taking out most of the money, Vincent left for Calgary with the package and two thousand dollars for Landsdown. Dalton also left him a thousand dollars to take care of business.

On his way back, Dalton met the second wagon train. They talked for a short while until Dalton rode out for the village with Thunderchild.

When Dalton arrived, he met with Raincloud.

"Only two of the five had their rifles painted. We have been watching every move of the remaining three."

"Anything suspicious?"

"Not yet" Raincloud replied.

As they walked, they came to the corral where two young groomers were looking after the horses taken from the McAllister gun fighters.

"You young fullas have sure done a good job of getting the grease off their legs" Dalton said.

"We worked on them for a whole day. We did not even know two of the horses had white socks until we got the grease off. We worked even harder on Chief Joseph's horse."

"Well, keep up the good work!"

As they walked, Raincloud stopped. He had his eyes wide open like a crazy man.

"Did you hear what he just said?!" Raincloud whispered.

"Yes. They cleaned up..." Dalton did not finish.

"We have to know when!" Raincloud said.

They went back and asked the boys what day they cleaned up Napoleon.

"It was early in the morning, just before Chief Joseph left for Calgary on the day of the massacre." The boy continued, "We thought it was mud but there was grease underneath."

The boys continued to groom as Dalton and Raincloud moved a few steps away.

"Did he bring his rifle to the forge to get it darkened?"

"Yes!"

"Position, jealousy and money" Dalton stated.

"Yes. I have heard him say several times that he would be Chief of Chiefs because he was the son of Chief Three Killer" Raincloud stated.

"We need one more thing. Was he gone from the village two days before the massacre?"

"It is him! The Flatheads could not see the white socks on his horse because they were covered with grease."

"Let us make sure!"

They returned to the corral and asked the boys if Joseph told him where he picked up all the grease.

"No" one of them answered.

"Yes" the other one replied. "He said he was out for small game near the lake."

"Do you know how many days he was out hunting?" Dalton asked.

"He was gone at least two days because the horse was gone that long. He always leaves his horse here in the corral."

Dalton and Raincloud looked at one another.

"We must pick him up" Raincloud said.

"First we must get these boys out of here. I do not want anyone talking to them."

Raincloud agreed and Dalton spoke to the boys.

"Now listen fullas, you have been working very hard with these horses. How would you like to ride the north trail and help out at the Strong Eagle Ranch?"

"That would be great!"

"Get your horses ready and meet us at the Wandering Buffalo Lodge."

"Maybe we should take two of these horses. They could use some work."

"Good idea. If you hurry, you can make it to the ranch for supper."

Dalton told Raincloud to pick up his two young riders and meet him and Thunderchild at the Wandering Buffalo Lodge.

Raincloud left immediately.

Wandering Buffalo was still shaking his head when Raincloud and the two riders arrived. Both of the young riders offered to kill Joseph immediately.

"This is the problem! If we tell what we know he will not make it through the day. We have to find out if there were other people involved" Dalton explained.

With some disappointment, everyone agreed.

"We should take him away from the village to question him" Raincloud said.

Just then, the two boys from the corral arrived and Thunderchild took them to the north trail.

It was agreed that Wandering Buffalo would ride three miles south on the Flathead Trail and set up camp with the two young riders and Thunderchild. An hour or two after they left, Raincloud and Dalton would pick up Joseph and take him to the camp.

Late in the afternoon, Dalton stopped Joseph just before he was about to enter the Great Hall.

"I would like to have a few words with you Joseph" Dalton stated.

"What about?"

"About the good job you are doing."

By this time, everyone was in the Great Hall. Raincloud drew his pistol and told him to shut up and move.

"We brought you a horse. Follow me!"

They turned the horses south and reached the camp in good time. The two young riders took their horses and tied them up.

"You killed four young men" Wandering Buffalo said.

"I did not kill anyone! What are you talking about?"

"You had the massacre arranged and that is the same thing as killing them!" Dalton exclaimed.

"McAllister and his gunfighters killed them. I was nowhere around."

Joseph was told the facts and he began to sweat and squirm.

"Before you die, I want you to tell us who else is involved." Raincloud stated.

"I have nothing to say. I am innocent."

"Would you like us to give you to the Flatheads? They just love people like you" Raincloud stated.

"No! No! I will tell you if you let me ride away. I will ride away and never come back."

"Go ahead! Tell us!" Dalton yelled.

Trembling and with a broken voice, Joseph began to talk.

"I was very jealous and angry when my father put you in charge of the council when he was dying. I knew then that I would not be made Chief of Chiefs."

"Who else is involved?" Dalton asked.

"I made friends with George Bull and Two Horns. Once you and Raincloud were out of the way, I knew I could take over the council. But you did not go with the wagons and Raincloud survived.

Once you and Raincloud were gone, I would pay Bull and Two Horns to bring in riders to take over the village. When this was done, I would leave for the East by train with my woman and the nation money."

"Anyone else?"

"No."

Dalton spoke to Raincloud and told him to take Joseph to the Flathead nation. He gave Raincloud fifty dollars for the Chief.

"Maybe there is someone else. If there is, they will find out. Tell them not to kill him! I will bring Victoria and they can die together."

Raincloud and his two riders left with Joseph to the Flathead nation.

Chapter Six

Kill the Slut

"That slut deserves to die. She helped kill four of my friends, including my brother."

The next morning, Dalton met with Victoria and asked her to ride South with him to look at a new trail through the Flathead Nation.

"Where is Joseph?" she asked.

"He went with Raincloud to talk with the Flatheads."

Thundercloud joined them and the three rode south. When they reached the Flathead Village, a warrior stopped them and pointed to a place west of the village. The three rode west and Dalton could soon see a group of warriors in the distance. They stopped where Raincloud and the two riders sat on the grass not far from the group of Flathead warriors.

"Did they find out anything from him?"

"We do not know. The Chief is the only one who speaks our language and a little bit of English. He saw you coming and will be here soon," Raincloud replied.

"Why are you sitting over here?"

"Go take a look and you will know."

Dalton saw the Chief coming and rode to where the Flathead warriors were gathered.

"What is going on?" Victoria asked.

"You will find out soon enough," Raincloud replied.

Dalton looked at Joseph who was buried up to his neck. His eye lids were slit and a piece of wood was wedged between his teeth and tied around his neck. Ants were crawling into his mouth, his eyes and into his ears.

The Chief arrived and Dalton asked him if there was anybody else.

"No. Just his woman and the other two."

"Bring Victoria down," Dalton ordered.

Victoria took a look at Joseph and was horrified at what she saw. She began yelling at Dalton and started calling him names. She went to her knees and put her hands over her face.

"Why?" she screamed.

"He is the traitor and you will die with him." Dalton drew his pistol and pointed it towards her head.

"Wait!" the Chief said, "She is not his woman!"

"Yes! She is his woman!"

"No! His woman is Cathy!"

There was a great silence. Even Victoria stopped yelling and cursing.

"My daughter! His stepdaughter!" Victoria exclaimed.

"Are you sure Chief?" Dalton asked.

"Yes, I am sure."

"This cannot be true," Victoria stated.

"How many times has Joseph gone to Calgary in the last four years?"

"Often," Victoria replied with a calm and steady voice.

"I do not know how we will make it up to you Victoria but we will," Dalton stated.

Dalton holstered his pistol and turned towards the Chief as Victoria went to her horse. In a split second, Dalton heard the blast as a bullet hit Joseph between the eyes. Dalton did not even turn around.

Victoria walked to where they stood.

"He was still my husband," Victoria said.

Dalton gave the Chief another fifty dollars and they all rode north towards the village.

No one spoke. Victoria rode between Raincloud and Dalton.

"Can we save her Chief Raincloud?"

"How?" Raincloud answered.

"Can we save her Chief Dalton?"

"How?" Dalton answered.

As they neared the village, Dalton explained that it was not over and no one in the village should know. They all agreed to meet after supper at the Wandering Buffalo Lodge.

"What a mess!" Victoria exclaimed.

That evening, the group met and tried to arrive at an answer for Victoria.

Dalton spoke. "Victoria wants to know if we can save her daughter. What is there to save? This is a person who is just as responsible for the massacre as Joseph. This is a person who betrayed her husband, mother and nation.

This is a person who, with the help of George Bull, Two Horns and their hired help, would kill more of the council. She is not even a mother! She planned to leave her son to be raised by his father while she left for the east with a traitor and nation money.

Now is there anyone here who can tell me why we should save her?"

Raincloud, who sat beside Victoria, hung his head and told the council he felt a little responsible because he brought Victoria and Cathy to the mountains when he returned from the Sioux Nation with his sister and her children.

Victoria put a hand on Raincloud's shoulder and shook her head.

"I brought my daughter here when she was eleven. Over the years, she grew up in a paradise while on the plains, many in the nations suffered. I do not know why she should live except to say that I am her mother.

The only thing that I can suggest is to pay her for her business and send her east to the Yankee Territory. That is where I am from and she has relatives there. Do not forget, she killed four of the white Police in the train robbery of eighty-three. How could she go to the Police?"

There was a great silence.

"What about George Bull and Two Horns?" Wandering Buffalo asked.

"What about Cathy?" Victoria demanded.

"We will return here in the morning and make our decision about Cathy," Dalton replied.

"George Bull and his friends should not be a problem," Raincloud stated.

"I do not think we have to kill everyone in his camp," Thundercloud offered.

"Why not?" Dalton asked.

"What Joseph and Bull planned would not be discussed with women and children and not with hired help. If we kill George Bull and Two Horns, the problem will just disappear," Thunderchild explained.

The council looked around and nodded their heads.

Once again, Dalton suggested that the Cathy and Bull decisions could wait until morning.

On the way out, Thunderchild motioned Dalton aside and spoke to him.

"I did not know the girl very much. I will kill her if you want, Chief Dalton."

Dalton hit Thunderchild on the shoulder and left for his lodge.

It was day fourteen and Dalton had to say yes or no in the morning.

After a good breakfast in the Great Hall, the group of seven walked to the Wandering Buffalo Lodge.

"How do we get Bull and Two Horns away from their camp?" Dalton asked.

"They sell stolen horses," Raincloud stated.

"Go ahead," Dalton said.

"We could send one of our two young scouts to speak with Bull. He will tell Bull that Wildfire sent him. They have two horses to sell but did not want to bring them to the camp. He would tell them the horses are tied by the River less than a mile away. We will really have the horses tied just in case they get suspicious. When they get close, we will kill them."

"What if they bring another rider or two?" Dalton asked.

"We will kill them too! Nobody is supposed to be friends with George Bull and Two Horns."

Everyone had a good laugh, even Victoria.

It was decided that the Raincloud plan was the way it would be done and he put Raincloud in charge.

Once again, there was a big silence.

"And Cathy?" Victoria asked.

"Did anyone speak with the creator last night?" Wandering Buffalo asked.

Everyone nodded their heads except one of the young riders.

"Did the Creator speak to you?" Wandering Buffalo asked.

Nobody answered.

Wandering Buffalo continued, "In the night, I saw a snake so big it could swallow a warrior. It brought other big snakes and they crawled along the ground killing our people that left the mountains. The Creator told me to kill this snake."

Victoria lowered her head and tears ran down her face.

Dalton got to his feet and left the lodge. Thunderchild followed him.

"Do you want me to do it, Chief Dalton?"

"No. I will do it," Dalton replied.

Thunderchild left and Victoria caught up with Dalton. He had tears in his eyes as Victoria spoke to him.

"What about Wildfire and the boy?"

"They must come to the mountains before I go to Calgary," Dalton replied.

"How will we do that?"

"Come back here at one o'clock. I do not wish to speak of it now."

"Maybe you should send someone else. It was Wandering Buffalo who had the dream."

Dalton shook his head and walked away.

Victoria had never seen him with tears and his head down. She felt sorry for Dalton as she watched him walk away.

When they returned at one o'clock, it was decided that a message for Wildfire would be delivered by Vincent instructing Wildfire to come immediately to the village for a few days to assist in planning for the McAllister massacre. The message also requested that he bring Timothy to visit with Victoria.

In the morning, Beth gave Dalton another package of three hundred applications, location of land purchases and five thousand dollars for him to give to Vincent.

"How much money is left in the nation?" Dalton asked.

"With eight thousand in total to Landsdown and expenses, we have, within a few hundred, fifty-one thousand dollars," Wandering Buffalo replied.

"I will withdraw what I have in Calgary and Beth can withdraw what she has in Lethbridge. We will bring the money here so we know what we have at all times."

"Yes. I will leave tomorrow morning with the wagons and bring the money to the village," Beth stated.

Dalton, Raincloud, Thunderchild and the two young scouts turned their horses north and headed for the Strong Eagle Ranch.

When they arrived at the Ranch, Dalton gave Vincent the package for Landsdown and the message for Wildfire.

Vincent left immediately to catch the afternoon train from Lethbridge to Calgary. Raincloud and his three riders got ready to leave for the George Bull Camp.

"When you are finished, come back to the ranch. I will meet you here when I return from Calgary."

"We will be here," Raincloud said.

Sarah and Heather went inside to prepare a meal before the wagons arrived.

As they sat around the table, Dalton explained the situation with Joseph and Cathy. When it got around to Cathy, Dalton lowered his head and did not speak.

"That slut deserves to die, she helped kill four of my friends including my brother. Let me go to Calgary, Chief Dalton!"

"When will you leave for Calgary?" Benjamin asked.

"I will leave when Wildfire arrives in the morning."

"How many of us will you need?" Sarah asked.

"I will go alone," Dalton replied.

The wagons soon arrived and Dalton left to say Hello.

Early in the morning, the wagons left for the village. Benjamin and Michael hooked up the covered buggy and left for Lethbridge to meet Wildfire. Sarah said she had a few things to pick up and left to saddle her horse. Dalton waited for her and the two rode east to catch up with the buggy.

The train was on time and Wildfire stepped down from the train with his son. Everyone took turns carrying Timothy around and talking to him about his first train ride.

"Benjamin will go with you to the village. The buggy can be returned to the ranch when the wagon train leaves in the morning," Dalton explained.

"Well, the village is a first for Timothy and I am looking forward to showing him off," Wildfire said.

"They will be glad to see you both."

Dalton met with Sarah and they went to the Hotel for dinner.

"How much money will you need for shopping?" Dalton asked.

"I have money, Chief Dalton."

"You know, I feel so bloody sorry for Wildfire. I have always liked him," Dalton said.

"This whole thing is just one big mess and thank God it will soon be over," Sarah stated.

Dalton spent a little time with Sarah and caught the one o'clock for Calgary.

When he arrived on the planks, Dalton spotted Vincent and followed him at a distance. They waited around a corner and discussed everything in detail.

"This is the horse I bought for getting around town. I tied the rifle on just in case you might need it. There is ammunition in the saddle bags for your colt and the winchester."

"I brought two thousand dollars with me from the nation. Give it to Landsdown. How are you fixed for money."

"I have enough money to last me for a while."

"Good! Get a horse from the livery and for the next day or so, make sure you are seen in town."

"The people in town are getting to know me. I give a little extra every now and then to those I buy from. They all call me Mr. Lugar."

"Somehow, that does not surprise me," Dalton said with a smile.

"Landsdown likes it when I meet with him. Every time I give him a few thousand dollars, he slams his fist on the table and says, Exemplary!"

"What does that word mean?" Dalton asked.

"I do not know but it must be good because when he says it, his mustache twitches and he gets a big shit eating grin on his face."

Dalton laughed for the first time in days.

"Leave my horse here when you are done. I will be looking for him."

Dalton nodded and rode west.

Chapter Seven

The Last of the Informers

"So he sent me here so he could kill my wife."

When Dalton reached the outskirts, he could see the Trading Post at the top of the slope, just a little west of the main road that ran north and south. He did not hurry for he wanted to return to Calgary just in time to catch the six o'clock to Lethbridge.

Dalton looked up and down the main road and with no one in sight, he took the west turn to the Trading Post. As he passed the sign which read "Dead End Trading Post," Dalton took a piece of paper from inside his coat and hammered it to the sign. It read, "Closed Until Monday."

As he rode through a small thicket of trees, Dalton walked his horse for the branches that hung over the trail caused a darkness that was peaceful. In just minutes,

Dalton was out of the trees and approaching the planks. He tied his horse and went inside.

There was no one in the front so Dalton walked to the living quarters. Cathy seemed busy drying large pots that she had laid out on the table.

"Chief Dalton!" she exclaimed as she turned around.

"Hello Cathy."

"What brings you to the Post?" Cathy asked.

"I was in Calgary doing a little business and thought I would drop by to say Hello before I left for Lethbridge."

"Can I make you something to eat?"

Dalton cleared his throat. "Joseph is dead. We took him to the Flathead Nation and on the way he told us about your plans. You were going to leave with him and without your son. He told us that he wished he had gone to the Police instead of returning to the mountains. We cannot have anyone talking to the Police."

Dalton reached under his coat to draw just as Cathy lifted a large lid and pointed her pistol at Dalton's head. She got off a shot and knocked Dalton to the floor. Blood poured from his head as she walked over to put another bullet in him.

Just as she was about to pull the trigger, Dalton hit her in the knee with his foot and the bullet hit the floor. Cathy stepped back and aimed again for Dalton's head. This time, a bullet came from the front room and hit Cathy in the throat. The bullet spun her around hitting the wall as she dropped her gun and grabbed her throat.

Dalton, who was on the floor and could not move, heard another blast that blew out the side of Cathy's head. Dalton saw a blurred figure move towards him.

"It is a good thing she hit you in the head."

"Jesus! Sarah!"

Everything turned black for Dalton as he lay on the floor.

Sarah raised Dalton from the floor and put a pillow under his head. She drew some cold water and cleaned the blood from his face and the wound. When the cold water hit, Dalton came around.

"This is a Trading Post! There must be liniment here!"

Sarah found what she was looking for and applied the liniment.

"What about salve?" Sarah exclaimed.

"There should be some here," Dalton stated.

Sarah looked at Dalton and smiled.

"I think you are going to live, Chief Dalton."

Sarah found the salve and put some on the wound. She then went up front and returned with a new shirt, jacket and hat.

"You saved my life, Sarah."

"We will talk later."

With a little help, Dalton raised himself from the floor and sat at the kitchen table. Sarah made coffee and found some soft biscuits.

As Dalton drank his coffee and ate biscuits, he looked at Cathy and shook his head. Sarah found a clean white cloth and tied it around Dalton's head to absorb the blood.

"How the hell did you get here from Lethbridge?" Dalton asked.

"We took the same train only I was a couple of coaches behind."

"Why did you come?"

"You just didn't look like you were ready to kill someone, Chief Dalton."

Dalton nodded his head.

"What are we going to do about her?" Sarah asked.

"Well, there is a little shack out back and down the slope. I will go a distance behind and dig a shallow grave. We will put her in it for she does not belong in the trees."

The two picked up shovels and headed towards the shack. The dirt was soft and in less than an hour, the grave was ready. They wrapped Cathy in a blanket and put her in the grave.

Dalton stretched his hands and looked upward. "Creator, this woman and mother betrayed her people, husband and son. Take her spirit to a good place for she was led down a crooked trail by an evil man."

"I will dig up some grass and plant it on the grave. By spring, you would not know there was a grave here."

Sarah cleaned up the Post while Dalton worked on the grave. She took clothes from the shelves and changed into clean riding pants and blouse.

When Dalton was finished, he took the shovels to the trough for cleaning. Sarah lit a fire and burned the soiled clothing as Dalton put the shovels where they belonged.

"I think most of the bleeding has stopped. I will clean the wound again and put on the salve," Sarah said.

After the wound was cleaned and everything burned, Dalton and Sarah left for the train. Dalton returned his horse to Vincent and Sarah returned her horse to the livery.

Sarah and Dalton sat in different seats as they took the six o'clock to Lethbridge.

When the train arrived, Sarah and Dalton picked up their horses at the livery and took the road west to the Strong Eagle Ranch.

"When will Raincloud be back?" Sarah asked.

"If everything goes right, they should return to the ranch before noon tomorrow."

"What will become of the Trading Post?" Sarah asked.

"Well, today is Saturday. Tomorrow Heather will take the evening train to Calgary and meet up with Vincent. They will open the Post Monday morning and operate it until we find out what Wildfire wants to do."

As they rode, their conversation got a little lighter. Dalton told Sarah about Landsdown and the "Exemplary" conversation. They were still laughing as they took the trail to the ranch.

When they arrived, supper was over. Some of the drivers were on the planks and some were in the barn. Sarah went inside while Dalton went from the barn to the planks speaking with the drivers.

"How many wagons have we got now?" Dalton asked.

"We have nine wagons now, Chief Dalton," a driver answered.

"We will have three more ready in a couple of days," another driver stated.

"Good! Our loads will be smaller when we start hauling the stones," Dalton added.

"But the money will be bigger." A driver exclaimed.

Everyone had a good laugh before Dalton was called inside for supper. When Sarah and Dalton were done eating, Gordon and Dalton took their mugs of wine to a small table beside the fireplace.

"Does anybody else but us few know what is going on?" Dalton asked.

"No. If anybody knew, the drivers would be talking," Dalton nodded.

"Is the Trading Post taken care of?" Gordon asked.

Dalton lowered his head and answered, "Yes. It has been taken care of."

Gordon reached over and put a hand on Dalton's shoulder. "It had to be done."

"I know," Dalton said in a whisper.

Dalton went on to tell Gordon what happened and he was surprised.

"Jesus! You would never know by looking at her that she was a killer. She killed Cathy to save your life. This whole thing could go down as self-defense."

Dalton nodded. "You know, Chief Dalton, with the hotel prices we are charging for meals, along with stables and feed for the horses, we are making a great deal of money."

"And the Nation will keep paying. We could not get along without your Ranch."

Gordon and Dalton finished their wine and went to the planks.

It was getting on to evening at the village and no one told Wildfire anything. Victoria and her two daughters, fifteen and seventeen, carried Timothy around showing him off to the village.

Wandering Buffalo came by and stopped in front of Victoria. He pointed with his nose towards Victoria's Lodge and she knew what he was saying.

"Now girls, I want you to take Timothy to the young warriors' camp on the upper levels and you will spend the night there with him. They know you are coming."

Victoria approached Wildfire and told him to visit with her in about an hour.

"I am going to soak in the hot water for a while," Victoria said.

"That sounds like a good idea! I am going to the small pool and I will meet you later."

Victoria returned to the Lodge just before dark and lit all the candles. The Lodge was very spacious and had a good sized bed for the two girls located behind a sheet of painted skins. There was a huge mattress off in a corner covered with buffalo blankets bottom and top. Each living area had a small stove. She did not bother to start a fire as it was a very hot day in July.

Victoria lit some candles which she placed on a small table by the fireplace along with two mugs and a bottle of wine. Wildfire soon arrived and was greeted with a hug.

"This sure is nice in here, Victoria."

"Yes, it will be a sad day for me and the girls when we leave."

Victoria added a little white whiskey to the bottle and filled up the mugs.

"This wine has a different taste," Wildfire said.

"Yes, we have added raspberry juice."

"It is very good."

Victoria kept filling the mugs and they talked mainly about the girls, Timothy and the Trading Post. Suddenly there was a silence.

"Joseph is dead. I killed him!"

"What did you say!"

"I said Joseph is dead. I killed him."

"My God, Victoria! Are you drunk?"

"I am getting there."

"Why did you kill him?"

"I killed him because he was the traitor."

"How do you know?" Wildfire asked.

"He confessed to Raincloud and Dalton."

"My God! Joseph! Your husband!"

"Why did he betray the nation? Why did he go to McAllister?"

"Because he was jealous of Dalton. He thought he should have been 'Chief of Chiefs.' Dalton was supposed to be with the wagons but he stayed behind to look after nation business. With Dalton and Raincloud out of the way, he could have taken over the council and with help from George Bull, Two Horns and hired guns, he would have taken over the village and the money."

"What was he going to do with all the money?"

"Steal it for him and another woman. The two of them would leave together for the east.

When he was being tortured by the Flatheads, he told them he should have reported everyone to the Police rather than return to the village."

"Why did the Flatheads have him?"

"Dalton wanted the truth."

"What about George Bull and Two Horns?" Wildfire asked.

"They are dead. Raincloud, Thunderchild and two young scouts left early this morning to kill them."

"How can you just sit there like nothing happened?"

"When I think of the four young warriors who were slaughtered, I do not have a problem with it and there are over a thousand people here who have to be put on the plains.

If Joseph and his woman went to the Police, many of us including Piapot, you and me would be hung. Do not forget, we slaughtered wolf hunters, whiskey traders, Blackfoot by the hundreds, and yes, even the white Police. You were there for that."

There was a silence.

"What about the other woman? Is she dead too?"

"Yes. Dalton took the one o'clock to Calgary and she is dead."

"Jesus! Who the hell was she?"

"Her name was Mrs. Cathy Wilde, with an 'e'."

Wildfire almost stopped breathing.

He said in a calm voice, "Are you talking about my wife and your daughter."

"Yes."

Wildfire got to his feet kicking his chair backwards against the wall.

"Woman, are you drunk! You are half crazy!"

"I am not drunk and I am not crazy. How many times did Joseph visit and how many times were you sent to the store?"

Wildfire picked up his chair and placed it back at the table. He grabbed his throat.

"So he sent me here so he could kill my wife!"

"Yes! We all agreed that you needed time to understand the truth! If you were told at the Trading Post, and you believed it and begged on your hands and knees, she would have laughed in your face. We all offered to kill her Wildfire! She was going east with Joseph and leaving you alone with Timothy just like you are right now!"

"How can you say these things about your own daughter? It is my place to kill my wife! I am going to kill that son of a bitch!"

"Dalton will not be back until tomorrow afternoon. You can kill him then. No one will try to stop you."

"Chief Piapot said you were a born killer. Just how cold hearted are you!"

"Think it through and quit whining! I lost an evil husband and an evil daughter. You just lost an evil bitch of a wife, Mr. Wilde!"

Wildfire grabbed Victoria by her blouse and raised his fist. Victoria did not flinch.

Wildfire got back in his chair and tears rolled down his face. Victoria picked the candle up from the floor and placed it on the table. She brought out soft biscuits and berries. Wildfire ate and said nothing.

She gave Wildfire a damp cloth and he wiped his face.

"We need rest. You can sleep in the children's bed or you can join me on the floor and we will talk."

Wildfire watched as she removed her cloth and crawled between the buffalo blankets. Her white hair glowed against the dark fur pillow as she folded the blanket down below her breasts. Victoria was a very beautiful woman.

Wildfire removed his cloth and crawled in beside her. It was not awkward for their loss drew them together. He reached down and moved his hand up and down the inside of her leg. Victoria spread her legs with great pleasure.

After they were exhausted, they held each other close knowing they found something good.

In the norming, Victoria was up and had two stoves burning. Pails of water steamed on top of the stoves. She mixed cold water with hot water and poked Wildfire with her foot.

They stood on spaced stones and laughed as they took turns pouring water. They used the white man's soap and it felt great.

After cleaning up, they crawled back under the buffalo robes.

"You know, if Dalton did not kill her I would have and right about now, I would be in jail waiting to be hung," Wildfire concluded.

When I told you to come to my lodge, I did not expect this to happen. Wandering Buffalo wanted you to know everything in order to give you time to think. This has been the best night and morning in my life. I do not know how it happened so fast."

"I am glad it did. I like you a lot, Victoria, but there is a ten year difference between us."

"Thirteen years," Victoria added.

"Does that bother you?"

"Not at all," Victoria replied.

"And do you promise to wake me up like this every morning?"

"As much as you want, whenever you want it."

Victoria crawled on top of Wildfire and gave it to him until sweat rolled down her back.

"I never believed it could be this good!" Victoria exclaimed.

Later in the morning, Wildfire and Victoria dressed and left for the Great Hall. They met Wandering Buffalo on the path and stopped to talk.

"Everyone is working very hard. What would you like me to do?" Wildfire asked.

"I take it you know about Cathy."

"Yes."

"What I would like you to do is enjoy the mountains with Victoria and the children."

"When will Chief Dalton return?" Wildfire asked.

"If everything goes right, he will return before supper."

Wildfire and Victoria left for the Great Hall to get something to eat before going to the young warriors' camp.

After a good breakfast, they walked to the upper level and met with the two girls and Timothy. The two girls were having fun playing mothers and Timothy was having a good time as well.

"Too bad we have to leave the mountains," Wildfire said.

"When Timothy grows up, maybe we will come back. This is where the last two hundred will live. The hot water to the village will be blocked but there will be hot water here."

"The pool up here is just as big as the one in the village," Wildfire said.

The two admired the view of the valley and spoke about their plans. Getting married would not be a problem as neither one of them were ever married.

"So we had better tell Beth to put the five of us down as the Wilde family after we get married tomorrow. There is a church near Cut Bank," Victoria said.

Wildfire agreed and the two walked back down to the village. Victoria was excited about having a real marriage and a real husband.

Chapter Eight

The Little White Church

"This is our first real marriages."

Back at the Strong Eagle Ranch, Dalton waited for Raincloud and his riders. It was day seventeen and Dalton hoped this would be the end of the killing. From a high place, Dalton saw riders approaching and he smiled as four riders leading three horses came into view.

Dalton rode down the slope whooping and hollering. There was much laughing and shoulder hits. Dalton was clearly pleased.

"We will go to the barn and give you a report," Raincloud said.

After the horses were fed and watered, the five sat cross legged in the straw as Raincloud gave an account of what happened.

"When we arrived at their camp, I sent Jonathan to talk to Bull. I told Jonathan that if Bull did not argue the price, it meant he was going to kill him when he saw the horses. Jonathan would ride to the right side of Bull if he did not argue the price. This we had to know so we could kill them maybe a little sooner than we planned.

Me and Thunderchild took the saddles and bridles off our horses and tied them to a tree. William stayed with the horses as I walked up one side of the trail and Thunderchild walked up the other side. We saw four riders approach and Jonathan rode on the right side of George Bull.

When they were close I nodded and we blew away the two riders that rode behind. When Jonathan heard the blasts, he shot George Bull in the side of the head. It was over in just a few seconds."

"Bull should have argued the price. They could have lived a few seconds more!" Dalton exclaimed.

Thunderchild laughed so hard he fell over backward.

After they all had a good laugh, Raincloud continued. "They were going to kill us all right. We went through their pockets and came up with just a little more than five dollars in coins. They had no intention of paying!

After we put them on their horses, we took them down the slope and threw them in the river. They are probably in Calgary by now."

There was more laughter.

"Do you think the people from the camp can back track you?" Dalton asked.

"No. We brushed away our tracks and did not take the trail. We rode through the trees and the high slopes. Their trail ends at the water."

"Well, we got rid of Bull, got three horses and saddles and five dollars. It was a good day's work."

"What about you, Chief Dalton. How did you make out in Calgary?" Thunderchild asked.

Dalton told them what happened.

"What the hell! You went to Calgary to speak with her about a relationship with Joseph and she tried to kill you. Sarah came along and saved your life! The whole thing sounds like self-defense!" Thunderchild exclaimed.

"Funny, that is what Gordon said. Anyhow, the nation killing is over and the McAllister massacre will start soon."

Dalton told Thunderchild to take the two scouts and take the six o'clock to Calgary with Heather to meet Vincent.

"It is important that you move Cathy away from the Trading Post and bury her a mile away. Bury her in the trees where a cow would not go. Take oil and burn the grave. Make sure she does not have anything on that will not burn. I would have done this myself but I was in no shape to do anything."

"We will take care of it, Chief Dalton," Thunderchild said.

Dalton left for the ranch house to speak with Michael and Sarah. He told them to saddle up and get ready to ride to the village.

"How long will I be at the Trading Post, Chief Dalton?" Heather asked.

"Just a few days. It will not take long to find out what Wildfire wants to do."

"Will Vincent be at the station?"

"Yes, he will meet the four of you at the station."

"I have not been to the Trading Post for a very long time. I had better take some money!"

Gordon and Dalton smiled.

"They like to spend," Gordon said with a shrug.

"Thunderchild and the two scouts will be back tomorrow to help out. We will take the three Bull horses to the village and leave three of our horses here just in case someone comes around."

"Good!" Gordon said.

Dalton and Raincloud grabbed a bite to eat and left for the village with Sarah and Michael.

"How many days has it been since the massacre?" Raincloud asked.

"Seventeen days," Dalton replied.

"It seems a lot longer."

"I know," Dalton stated.

"This has been the worst massacre we have seen. In the other massacres, we knew our enemies. I am glad it is over," Raincloud stated.

"It is not over yet. We have Wildfire to deal with," Sarah added.

Raincloud looked at Dalton.

"You are going to have to get used to her. She has opinions," Dalton said.

"Let me say this. We have been through a lot and if Wildfire shoots off his mouth, I will put a bullet between his eyes!" Raincloud exclaimed.

"No! No! Let me handle this! When we get to the village, you and Michael go soak in the warriors' pool."

"That sounds good to me! Right, Michael?"

"Right!" Michael agreed.

"Do you want to soak with us, Sarah?" Raincloud asked.

"And get a bullet between my eyes!"

This brought much laughter as they picked up the pace for the village.

When they reached the village, the four went straight to the corral and gave their horses to several buck warriors. Michael and Raincloud left for the warriors' pool and Sarah ran to meet her mother, Anne, and her father, Big Man Walking. Dalton watched as she was met with hugs and kisses.

"The Walkers," Dalton said to himself.

Dalton turned and went to where Wandering Buffalo was waiting.

"What do you think of your granddaughter?"

"She is beautiful like her mother and grandmother."

Dalton told Wandering Buffalo about Cathy and how Sarah saved his life. Wandering Buffalo told him it sounded a lot like self-defense.

"What about Bull, Chief Dalton?"

"Yes. He is dead along with Two Horns and one other rider," Dalton answered.

"My Lord! It is over!"

"Not quite! Sarah says we still have Wildfire to deal with."

Wandering Buffalo gave Dalton a curious look.

"You are going to have to get used to your granddaughter. She has opinions." Dalton shrugged his shoulders.

The two left in different directions just as Wildfire walked down the path to the corral.

"Chief Dalton!"

Dalton stopped and watched as Wildfire approached. When he was in front of Dalton, Wildfire spoke.

"Is she dead?"

"Yes, she is dead," Dalton said in a whisper.

"It was my place to kill her!" Wildfire exclaimed.

"No. It was up to the nation. No man should be asked to kill his wife."

"When I heard you went to Calgary, I wanted to kill you."

Dalton moved his shoulders to the left and drew his colt from the left holster. Wildfire saw it coming and reached down to draw. His pistol hardly cleared the holster before Dalton shoved the steel into his chest.

Dalton grabbed the right arm of Wildfire and shoved the butt end of his colt into Wildfire's hand.

"You can kill me if you like Wildfire. I just do not care anymore."

Dalton turned and walked towards his lodge. Wildfire called his name and told him to stop. Dalton stopped as Wildfire walked towards him. He stopped in front of Dalton and gave him back his colt.

"I am sorry, Chief Dalton."

Dalton holstered his colt and put both arms around Wildfire.

"Maybe there is some good news," Wildfire said.

"Jesus! If there is good news, let's hear it!"

"Me and Victoria will try to make a family."

Wandering Buffalo, who was hidden behind small brush, lowered his winchester and went to meet his granddaughter.

"Tomorrow we are going to the little white church north of the Snake. We will ask the priest to marry us."

"I know the church," Dalton said.

"We want you and Little Tree to come with us."

"We will come and there will be two weddings. Little Tree has always wanted us to get married."

Wildfire left to tell Victoria and Dalton went to his lodge.

Before Little Tree could even put food on the table, Dalton took off his boots and fell asleep on the Buffalo robes.

"How are we going to explain Joseph to the girls?"

"I have been thinking about that. Tell the girls Joseph was in the south tracking the traitor. He tried to cross the Snake and drowned in the white water."

"I guess that is about as good as anything else," Victoria agreed.

"I will take Timothy and you can spend the rest of the day with the girls. I will spread this story in the village and join the three of you later in the day."

After a couple of hours sleep, Dalton ate a small meal and told Little Tree they were getting married. He told her about Victoria, Cathy and Joseph. Little Tree had tears of joy and sorrow.

"I will put new clothes together for this special occasion," Little Tree said.

"I will have two packhorses ready in the morning, one loaded with jars of food for the priest and one for us. We are going to camp and spend the night under the stars just like old times."

"I will tell Victoria to bring the girls. It will be good for them," Little Tree continued. "I think it will be a good marriage for Victoria. Timothy is her grandson and the girls are aunts. It is almost a family already."

Dalton nodded and left for a council meeting.

"A little while ago, one of the riders from the wagon train rode straight back from Lethbridge with a package from Vincent."

Beth opened the package for all to see. The package contained the Canadian identification for the first two hundred applications and there were also titles to land.

Everyone got to their feet and there was much whooping and hollering.

"I was beginning to wonder about this Landsdown!" a young counselor exclaimed.

"Now I really feel like working," Beth continued. "Our young warriors will organize the first two hundred first thing in the morning and move them out two days from now."

"Tell us about the cost, Beth," Dalton said.

"Not everyone is going to ranch or farm. Here is a piece of paper that will give us the approximate cost."

Dalton read what was on the paper.

1. $25.00 for each man, woman and child $5,000.00
2. 16 quarters of land $640.00
3. Fees to Landsdown $3,600.00
4. One large piece of luggage for each adult $500.00
5. One small piece of luggage for each child $250.00
6. $5.00 each for travel by train $375.00

$10,365.00

Also, those who must travel by train will be paid for their horses and possessions left behind. This is not an expense because we can sell the horses to ranchers and other possessions can be sold at the Wilde Trading Post in Calgary.

"In other words, it will cost the nation about $100.00 per person. Is that correct?" Dalton asked.

"That is correct, Beth answered.

"How much money have we got right now, Big Man Walking?" Dalton asked.

"I am now James Walker."

There was laughter and shoulder hugs for Big Man Walking.

"James continued, "Well, there will be about 225 over fifty-five years old who wish to remain in the mountains. So about 800 will be leaving and it will cost the nation $80,000.00. Here is another piece of paper that shows how much money we have in the nation.

Dalton read what was on the paper.

Cash remaining here	$47,000.00
Dalton cash in Calgary	$10,000.00
50 loads to Landsdown	$8,000.00
Money paid to Landsdown	$5,000.00
	$70,000.00

Also, we must continue to pay for meals and feed but we still have lumber and stones to haul. I estimate that the nation will have a small amount of money when everything is finished.

Dalton banged his fist on the table and hollered "Exemplary! Mr. Walker!"

Everyone had heard the story and there was a roar of laughter and shoulder hits.

Dalton told everyone that he would be gone tomorrow and return before noon on the second day.

"Where are you going, Chief Dalton, or is it a secret?"

"Me and Wildfire are going to get married to our women in the little white church."

This brought everyone to their feet asking questions of all kinds. Dalton had never seen people so excited.

"This is our first real marriages!" one of them shouted.

"Yes! And we will delay sending the two hundred for another day. There is going to be a great feast!"

"We will stop the wagons tomorrow and delay tearing down the Great Hall and big swimming pool. This is good news for our mountain people, Chief Dalton!" Wandering Buffalo exclaimed.

Dalton left and met with Victoria and Wildfire. They were as excited as everyone else. Victoria told Dalton about the Joseph story.

"That will be all anyone has to know," Dalton continued. "What about Cathy?"

"Cathy left for the east with a supplier. There were rumors anyhow," Wildfire said.

Dalton nodded and left for his lodge.

Chapter Nine

The Wedding Celebration

"Our French girls sure as hell know how to make pies!"

After a good night's sleep, Dalton felt rested and ready to ride. When Little Tree and Dalton reached the corral, the young groomers had the packhorses loaded and their horses saddled. The Wilde family was waiting and the six of them left for the church. It was only a four-hour ride so they took their time and enjoyed the foothills.

They arrived at the church before noon and they were greeted by Father Dupuis.

"We have brought some provisions and two small kegs of wine," Dalton said.

"Wine?"

"Yes, one for you."

"Well, let us get that keg inside and try it out!" Father Dupuis exclaimed.

Wildfire stoked up the big stove and the girls hauled in the provisions and one keg.

"We will make some bread and fresh berry pies," Victoria said.

"Oh! How magnificent!"

"There is feed for the horses in the barn and a corral out the back door," Father Dupuis offered. Dalton left to look after the horses.

When Dalton returned, Wildfire opened the keg and gave Father Dupuis a mug full.

After a taste of the wine, Father Dupuis smacked his lips and his eyes lit up.

"There is something different and very tasty about this wine."

"Yes. We added raspberry juice," Dalton stated.

"How Magnificent!"

Everyone laughed.

When the baking was finished and the table set, Dalton told Father Dupuis why they came.

"Are you all good Catholics?"

"Oh, yes!" they all said at once.

The Father smiled. "Well, you are all good Catholics today and that is what counts. When we are done eating, I will get right to it."

When he was done, Father Dupuis left for the church while the rest took turns changing their clothes. The six of them were ready in just a few minutes and they walked to the church.

Candles were lit and the grooms and brides took their vows. The only name change on the documents was a name change for Little Tree. She became Louise Dillon.

There was an older Father present who witnessed the documents and hauled out a camera.

"Now! You four stand and the girls will sit in front on these two chairs."

Wildfire hauled the chairs over and the camera flashed several times.

"I will have these ready for you by morning."

They were all excited about seeing the pictures.

Dalton and Wildfire called Father Dupuis aside and gave him twenty dollars.

"This is far too much!"

"Not at all!" Dalton said.

The two gave Father Dupuis a shoulder hug and left with the girls to find a nice place to camp. They found a grassy place between two stands of cedars. It overlooked a valley with a small river that ran down into the Snake. Victoria's daughters just loved the location.

Dalton walked back to the corral and returned with one of the packhorses. They unloaded everything and Dalton returned the packhorse to the corral.

When he got back, Wildfire had already dug some dirt up and the girls were putting stones around the hole. They gathered wood and lit a small fire. The wood kept coming and was piled to one side. Louise and Victoria took the large grill and fry pans out while Dalton and Wildfire spread the six buffalo robes.

"We have six beautiful deer steaks. Tonight will be a feast of deer steaks, fried potatoes and Piapot beets," Louise said.

"Let's get that keg of wine open!" Victoria exclaimed.

They filled up four mugs and the two young daughters passed out soft biscuits. Louise played her guitar and they sang songs in French and English. The daughters danced to Wildfire's small drum.

Toward evening, they cooked their steaks and the four women took the dishes to the barn for cleaning.

"Did you tell the girls about their father?" Dalton asked.

"Yes. They cried but their father was not around very much. If we can keep having this much fun, they will soon forget," Wildfire replied.

"I think it will be even better when you get back to the Trading Post," Dalton added.

Wildfire nodded.

As evening came, the two girls crawled into their buffalo robes with Dalton and Louise on one side and Wildfire and Victoria on the other.

Dalton lifted his mug. "Here's to the Wildes!"

Wildfire raised his mug. "Here's to the Dillons!"

They had a good laugh and crawled into their robes.

Morning was full of excitement. The four girls ran to the church to look at the pictures. Dalton and Wildfire went to the barn and got the horses ready. In a few minutes, the girls ran to the barn waving the pictures. They all spoke at once.

The pictures are magnificent! Good Lord, I am sounding like Father Dupuis now!" Victoria exclaimed.

As they turned around, the two Fathers stood there smiling.

"I think you are going to have a few more marriages to perform, Father Dupuis!" Louise exclaimed.

"They will all be very welcome."

The wedding party waved as they disappeared over the slope.

Four hours later, the wedding party arrived at the village. The two girls ran to meet their friends and many followed as the wedding party rode to the corral. The groomers took the six horses for feed and water while the newlyweds spoke to the crowd.

Victoria showed the wedding pictures and some of the women cried.

"Do not worry! Father Dupuis says he will marry you all!" Louise exclaimed.

"What did you have to do?" one of them asked.

"We just repeated what he said and the Father pronounced us man and wife. We signed a book and he gave us papers with his signature as proof of our marriage."

Victoria and Louise left for their lodges. Dalton and Wildfire went to meet with Wandering Buffalo.

"So, what is your new name, Wandering Buffalo?" Dalton asked.

"I am George Buffalo. I wrote myself as metis so I could have the same rights as Canadians. You never know when I might want to go to Calgary for a beer."

"Well, I guess we will soon call ourselves by our first names. When everyone is gone, there will be no need for so many chiefs, I will be called just Joseph," Dalton stated.

"Even though there will be only two hundred of us left in the mountains, you will always be called Chief Dalton until the day you are no longer with us."

Dalton nodded his head and smiled.

"I want a meeting in the warriors' room tomorrow morning with just the Chiefs, Sarah, Michael and the Wildes."

"The Wildes! It sounds good, Chief Dalton," Wildfire said.

Dalton and Wildfire left to meet with their wives.

The next morning, in the warriors' room, the conversation moved along to McAllister.

"It has been nineteen days since the massacre and it is time to deal with McAllister. Only me and the best of the dog warriors will go into the Yankee Territory to deal with McAllister and his hired guns.

I will need a family to gather information just like Piapot did when he took the elders to his reserve. My son, Michael, will be one for he is as white as me. I cannot go because I did business with McAllister. My choice for a second person is Sarah and for the mother, it will have to be Anne or Victoria.

Victoria and Wildfire should return to the Trading Post as soon as possible. I want them to leave tomorrow. It will be up to the Walkers to allow Sarah and Anne to join Michael."

"I am going. He was responsible for killing my brother and his friends!" Sarah exclaimed.

"I will go because I am Sarah's mother and it will look just that much more natural."

"Now I do not want any killing down there unless it is necessary. We need information only," Dalton added.

"I think this would be a good family for our daughter and granddaughter do look alike," Wandering Buffalo stated.

Wandering Buffalo looked at Beth, wanting her to speak.

Beth nodded her head. "I want the three of you to be careful. I will pray for you."

"Now that you are all here, I will tell you what Chief Piapot said about the money. He told me to spend what is necessary to put our people on the plains. Whatever is left, is to be divided equally among each man and woman who will remain in the mountains."

"I do not think there will be very much," James Walker added.

"We do not need very much," George Buffalo replied.

"There may be more than we think! Do not forget, we intend to take all of McAllister's money including his horses and cattle. It is almost noon and I hear the drums. Let us have a good time today and we will meet here tomorrow at one o'clock."

When they were leaving, Beth took Wandering Buffalo aside. "So?" she asked.

"What? What do you mean?"

"So when are we going to the little white church? It has been over thirty years you know."

"You have a fine white name. You want to be a Buffalo now?"

"Yes! Mrs. George Buffalo! Beth Buffalo! It sounds so wonderful!"

"When we are done here with the work, we will go to the little white church."

George caught Beth as she leaped towards him. The two left, laughing and hugging as they walked.

Drums pounded and there were groups here and there playing guitars and mouth organs. Women met in groups and spoke of the little white church. The wedding party appeared on the planks dressed in their wedding clothes and Wildfire spoke to the crowd.

"Me and Victoria have become a family."

There was hollering and the crowd shouted, "The Wildes!" "The Wildes!"

"You have all heard that Joseph was lost in the white water and Cathy left for the east with another man. I am glad she left for my family is bigger and I have much in my heart for Victoria."

The crowd roared their approval.

"As Chief of Chiefs, I want everyone to eat and enjoy the nation's new wine."

The crowd hollered, "Raspberry! Raspberry!"

Dalton continued, "My wife, Little Tree, is now Louise Dillon. This will be the last feast for the nation but for those of you who find your way back to the mountains, the dog warriors will be waiting for you."

The crowd roared as the wedding party stepped down from the planks and mingled with the people. Fish, steaks and potatoes were cooking on the planks. Baskets of berries, soft biscuits, along with jars of vegetables were placed on tables. Kegs of wine were opened for those who liked wine.

Late in the afternoon, the organ and piano were uncovered and Piapot's grandchildren played for the crowd.

Dalton and Wandering Buffalo took their turns step dancing and were cheered on by the crowd. Music and food was everywhere.

"Our French girls sure as hell know how to make pies!" Dalton exclaimed.

Gordon Strong and Benjamin Stonebreaker talked as they listened to the music.

"I will not go with you in the morning. Chief Dalton has put me in charge of the Great Hall tear down and closing off all the hot water that comes down from the warriors' camp," Benjamin said.

"Yes. It has been a great feast and I will leave with the wagons in the morning. Too bad Vincent and Heather could not come," Gordon added.

"Not tomorrow but the next day, the Wildes will return to the Trading Post," Benjamin stated.

"It will be good to get my wife back."

As evening came, the crowd got smaller. Some sat in groups around small fires and others went to their lodges. Over fifty men and women were busy cleaning outside and inside the Great Hall.

In the morning, the wagons that were loaded the day before, left for Lethbridge just before noon. The two scouts returned from Calgary and had a parcel from Vincent. Beth opened the parcel and found three hundred Canadian certificates and land titles.

The news of the parcel was in the village as Dalton walked to the warriors' room. Everyone arrived at 11 o'clock.

"We have three hundred more completed applications and the land titles. The assistants are busy right now giving the first two hundred what they need," Beth exclaimed.

"Benjamin will be in charge of the remaining tear-downs. There is hot and cold water lines involved and that is why he is here. Tomorrow I will go as far as Calgary with the Walker family and the Wildes.

The Walker family will take five hundred dollars and travel east by train. They will then go south and approach the McAllister settlement from the east. Gordon will receive their telegrams sent to Lethbridge.

When I get to Calgary, I will close my account and give ten thousand dollars to Landsdown. This will give us a credit to date."

The meeting ended and everyone left.

Chapter Ten

The Trading Post

"How does all the water get to all the rooms?"

The next morning, people were on the move. Those who were going to Calgary and Lethbridge to work for Landsdown left on horseback. They were paid money to buy luggage at the Trading Post in Calgary and Lethbridge.

Half the wagons hauled the Wildes and the Walker family along with those who would take the train to their reserves. The wagons arrived at Lethbridge on time and the five wagon loads of people took the six o'clock to Calgary. Dalton took his horse to the livery.

When they reached Calgary, Vincent had a horse waiting for Dalton and a wagon for the Wildes. They all left for the Trading Post where Heather had food on the table. As they came through the door, Dalton gave Heather a hug and sat down at the table.

"Well, how have sales been?" Wildfire asked.

"We have been very busy. I think we have purchased all the luggage in Calgary. We have more coming by train in a couple of days," Heather stated.

"I know you sold a lot of luggage because I saw the wagons unload it all," Wildfire said.

After supper, Victoria carried Timothy around while the girls started looking at everything in the Trading Post. It was an exciting time for them.

The men sat outside on the planks while Victoria and Heather cleaned up the kitchen.

"I guess you know everything about Joseph and Cathy," Victoria said.

"Yes. I will show you and Wildfire where she is buried when the time is right."

Victoria nodded.

"We will take the wagon back to the livery and I will stay with my sister tonight and catch the morning train to Lethbridge," Heather stated.

"Yes. I guess Vincent and Dalton will stay at the boarding house tonight."

After everyone said their goodbyes, the three left for Calgary. Victoria and William sat out on the planks and discussed their plans, including living quarters.

"Until we can build a house near the Post or build on to the Post, we will give our bedroom to the girls," William stated.

"Where will we sleep?"

"We will have to make do by sleeping in the business quarters."

"Marvelous! We can keep our eye on the goods at the same time!" They both had a good laugh.

"We owe Vincent and Heather for looking after the Trading Post," Victoria said.

"Yes. Vincent has been looking at these boots and Heather and her girls will be back soon to shop. You will make sure she gets a nice gift."

Victoria nodded.

"How much do we owe on the Post?" Victoria asked.

"Less than two hundred dollars."

"And how much do we owe the bank?"

"Again, less than two hundred dollars."

"Well, Mr. Wilde, with what I got from the nation along with payment for horses, personal items, and money in the bank, I have more than five hundred dollars."

"That much!" William exclaimed.

"Yes! We will pay off the debt and start saving for a house. My name will be on all of the papers including this Trading Post."

William smiled and nodded his head.

"We should make use of the bedroom before we move it," Victoria whispered.

"Where are the kids?" William asked.

"The girls took Timothy to the barn to play."

Wildfire agreed that it would be some time before they had any privacy and followed Victoria to the bedroom.

In the morning, Vincent sent a telegram to the Fort while Dalton went to the bank. The telegram read: Buildings torn down . . . . mice on the prairie . . . . rats poisoned.

The two met at the lodge where Landsdown joined them for breakfast.

"My supplier sure likes the way your workers get things done," Landsdown stated.

"And we would like to thank you for putting our men to work on your construction sites," Dalton added.

"You keep sending them."

After breakfast, the three proceeded to a private room. Dalton emptied his saddle bags on the table and placed ten thousand dollars in front of Landsdown.

"My good Lord! How much is here?" One side of Landsdown's moustache began to twitch.

"Ten thousand dollars! And here are the remainder of the applications and land locations. I would like you to keep things moving along as fast as possible."

Landsdown had a big shit-eating grin on his face and his moustache began to twitch on both sides as he banged his fist on the table and shouted, "Expeditiously, Mr. Dillon!! Expeditiously!!"

Vincent and Dalton held back their laughter and shook hands with Landsdown as he left the boarding house with a briefcase full of money.

As the door closed behind him, Dalton bent over laughing and backed into a large chair. Vincent pounded his fist of the table and kept repeating, "Expeditiously, Mr. Dillon!"

"What the hell did he say, Vincent?"

"I do not know but I think it is good!"

It took a while for the two to settle down as they finally agreed that Landsdown was going to move with great speed.

"I wonder if Landsdown knows how much fun we are having with him?" Vincent asked.

"I hope he never finds out!" Dalton replied.

The two got themselves together and rode to the station. The train arrived in a few minutes and six builders from the village stepped down to the planks.

"Are the building materials on the train?" Dalton asked.

"Yes. The boxcar is side-tracked just south of the livery," one of them replied.

"Good! A few of the ranchers who came from our village will be here soon with wagons. Do you have the plans for the house, Grey Owl?" Dalton asked.

"I am now James Grey."

There was laughter and shoulder hits.

"I do not think I am ever going to get used to all these fancy names. I am losing all my friends," Dalton said.

They all went to the livery where James explained the plans. The Post would be gutted back to the kitchen and twelve by twelve's would support the ceiling beams where the partitions were removed. The pump in the kitchen will remain. An extra pump will be put down to take water to the new rooms.

"You are going to take water into the rooms?"

"Yes. Benjamin Stonebreaker made these plans," James stated.

"If Benjamin Stonebreaker says it can be done, then it can be done!" Vincent exclaimed.

Everyone laughed at Vincent and nodded.

"Now the Post runs east and west," James continued. "We will build north to south in a straight line even with the east wall of the Post.

If you are in the kitchen and dining room area looking south, there will be a fireplace near the center of the wall and a five foot hallway running south almost to the end of the new building. The wall to the right of the hallway will be the outside wall with two windows side by side.

On the other side of the hall will be three bedrooms. The first bedroom will be about twelve by twelve, the second bedroom for Timothy will be ten by twelve and the third bedroom for the girls will be fourteen by twelve.

The small bedroom will not have heating. Instead, three square holes will be left near the top of the north and south wall and this will be enough heat.

Now, let me explain the fireplace that will heat the water. We have built a steel box divided in two and open at the top. Once we have the stones raised and leveled, we will place the steel box inside. One half will be for the fire and the other half will hold water that will be heated by the hot steel divider.

If you are in the bedroom, the back plate will be very hot and it will heat your room without making a fire. Less mess!"

They all nodded their heads and moved closer to see the plans.

James continued, "Now to the left of the fireplace, we will build a counter for the basin, water container and place a mirror on the wall. Now this room is complete."

"Tell us about the water!" one of them exclaimed. "How does the water get to all the rooms?"

"I could use a drink of raspberry wine!"

"There is no time. I will send up a barrel when I get back to the mountains. Tell us about the water," Dalton said.

James continued, "Let us now go to the kitchen. To begin with, we have taken a small piece of cedar log not very round and cut in half. Now we cut both halves with a saw like a 'V' and removed the pieces. We put them back together and tied them with rawhide. This small sleeve is hung over the spout, for what reason?"

Nobody answered.

"When the water comes out, it will go down the sleeve onto another half cut-out piece of cedar without splashing all over the kitchen."

"How does the water get to all the rooms?"

"It is simple. The cut-out trough goes through the stone wall and rests on top of the steel container. Now the steel container will have a small half circle hammered over just like the spout on the pump. When the container fills, it will overflow into another one-piece trough which goes through the first and second bedrooms. We will put a finishing around the holes in the wall. Now at the end of the small bedroom, the floor will be lowered two steps, for two reasons. To begin with, the one-piece trough is not long enough to continue through the girls' room so we have to place another one-piece trough under the long trough to take the water along to the steel container on the other side of the south wall.

Also, if we did not lower the floor, the ceiling would be too low as the roof will slope from north to south.

Before I continue, I will tell you that there are short troughs bolted to the ends of both troughs leading to the containers. These short troughs will be cut on top and may be folded up or down. This will allow you to take the water directly past the containers when they are down or into the containers when they are up."

"Of course!" Vincent exclaimed.

"What about the water in the girls' room? Will it not overflow?" Dalton asked.

"Let me finish. The end of the hallway is not the end of the building. The door you see at the end leads to a coal and wood room.

Then to the left is another door leading to the other side of the coal and wood partition. Now open the door and you will be standing in the last room. This room is fifteen feet by twelve feet. There will be a twelve and a half foot partition dividing the room. And there will be a seven foot partition on the north end which now makes a room twelve and a half feet by seven feet. This room is divided by a partition that makes this room five and a half feet by seven feet. The entire floor will be flat stone.

The five and a half foot room will have a small door on the right which will take you inside where there is a five foot white man's tub against the east wall.

Now, you asked about the water overflowing in the girls' room. The fireplace and water tank is located in front of the small room where the white man's tub is located. There is a distance of two and a half feet between the north end of the small room and the south end of the girls' room. There is a spout in the tank just like the one in the first room. This will take the overflow into a solid trough that takes the water along the east wall, through the room with the tub and through the partition a few inches into the other room and empties into a wooden barrel. This is where the water ends.

Now, in the tub room, the trough will have a plug. When the plug is removed, the tub will fill. The tub will have a plug and when the plug is removed, the water will fall on a slanted area which has a hole that takes the water down into a pipe that runs about eleven feet west into the main sewer. When the barrel in the other room is full, it will overflow through a notched out piece on top onto a slanted area and underneath the partition dividing the two rooms. The water will go down the same drain as the tub room and end up in the main sewer.

"This is amazing," Dalton exclaimed. "Tell us about the other room!"

"Now again, let us go through the door from the hallway and turn right. At the end of the five-foot hallway will be two latrines. They will be divided by a three-foot partition and have two doors like a saloon."

They all looked at one another.

"There will be a two-foot door going into the other room. Beside the door is another two-foot steel fireplace set back with a flat top. When the fireplace is fired up, this room will get very hot.

If you want steam, take two pails of water from the barrel and place them on the flat steel. You will have as much steam as you want. There will be a small door so anyone in the tub room can reach in and take pails of hot water to make the water in the tub just right."

"Good Lord! I must have this for my house!"

Everyone turned around.

"Sam! Have you been listening all the time?"

"You bet I have! Now I have treated you fullas pretty good around here. Anything you ever wanted in my livery, I gave you for a fair price. Me and the wife have been married for over forty years and she deserves something like this. I want to be first on your list after the Trading Post! Money is no problem!"

"How do you know this is going to work?" Dalton asked.

"Because Benjamin Stonebreaker said so!"

This brought a roar of laughter.

Dalton gave Sam a hit on the shoulder and promised him he was next.

"Now you move in here real close, Sam."

Sam moved right in between Dalton and Vincent.

"I just want to finish up. Now in the steam room up on the north wall just a little higher than you, Chief Dalton, a cedar box, closed on all four sides, will be installed. It will have holes in it so you can pour water in and let it drip down. You can use the white man's soap and clean up while you steam. The steel pails of water will be too hot to lift, so pour water from the pail and water from the barrel into a cedar pail until you get it just right. Now you can use the cedar pail to pour the water into the box.

Let me tell you about the sewer. We will lift a few planks and the sewer will begin in the kitchen. It will run north to south ending just below the stall on the right. The sewer will have a steep grade allowing water to flow very fast. Pipes will connect to the sewer at a slight angle from the two bedrooms, the tub room and the kitchen.

The end of the sewer will drop the water down into a lower and bigger sewer that runs under both stalls. The big sewer will be graded and carry all the waste away from the Post to a low place.

With all the water travelling towards the stalls, there should be no problem with waste. There will be cedar plugs placed on the bedroom and the tub room drains after use just in case of smell.

Now, the builders use what is called shavings to keep in the heat. We have more shavings than we will ever use. The wagons will send us potato bags full and we will insulate the walls and the ceiling.

What I like most of all about the Benjamin plan is the last room. With the two fireplaces, it will be very warm.

Do you have any more questions?"

Everyone spoke at once. They all wanted to know when it would be finished. With more help on the way, James told them it would take less than twenty days.

"I will go to the post and let them know what is happening," Dalton said.

Dalton arrived at the Post just before noon and sat down at the kitchen table with Victoria and Wildfire. He told them about the addition the best he could.

"James will be here soon and explain everything in detail," Dalton stated.

"We do not have the money," Victoria said.

"The nation considers this an investment. Do not forget that we have many wagon loads of goods to bring from the mountains. We will send them here by train from Lethbridge and you will sell them.

If you pay us the money you collect, we will consider your bill for the addition paid in full. Do we have a deal?"

"Do we have a deal!? You bet we have a deal!" Wildfire exclaimed.

"This is too much, Chief Dalton," Victoria added.

Dalton disagreed and left to catch the southbound.

Chapter Eleven

The Tear Down

"I am concerned about the police finding this village before we are finished"

Dalton arrived in Lethbridge and after getting his horse from the livery, he headed for the Gordon Stone Ranch. On the way, he met the wagons loaded with people and product. He spoke with the drivers and rode west to the ranch.

When he reached the ranch, people were busy getting ready for the drivers and horses.

"Have you had dinner, Chief Dalton?" Heather asked.

"No! I am hungry as a bear!"

Heather took Dalton inside and made him something to eat. The two sat at the table and talked while Dalton finished his meal.

"Are you staying the night?" Heather asked.

"No. I just stopped by to say Hello and grab a bite before leaving for the village. How are you fixed for money?"

"Just fine. Vincent paid me up to date before I left on the train. Also, I have a telegram for you."

Heather left and returned with the telegram. She gave it to Dalton and he read it for Heather to hear. "Three to the settlement in two days."

"I will be happy when they get back to the village," Heather said.

"Me too!"

Dalton left for the barns and spoke with the workers before he mounted up and rode south.

It was after six o'clock when Dalton reached the village. There was a lot of activity as people were preparing to leave. Benjamin Stonebreaker and Wandering Buffalo spotted Dalton and walked to meet him as two young groomers took his horse to the corral.

"All the stones from pools have been removed and just about all the buildings have been taken down," Benjamin stated.

"Tomorrow we will start taking down the Great Hall. Let us go there and have one last meal and wine," Wandering Buffalo added.

"That sounds good to me!" Dalton exclaimed.

As they ate and drank wine, Benjamin was asked to explain just how the village would look when everything was done.

"When everything is done, the rock forge will be the only building standing. It is empty now. Most of the equipment went to Calgary and the rest we have taken to the upper levels where we will build a small forge. You and the dog warriors will need it for shoeing horses and for other small jobs.

We will move some of the stoves into the empty forge tomorrow morning to cook for the workers. Everyone else will cook outside just like the old days. When everyone leaves, the forge will remain to make this village look like an abandoned camp site used by the mixed bloods for trapping and hunting. We have several wagons that are of no use. They are stripped down and old. These wagons will be placed here and there for the same reason that we are leaving the forge standing."

By this time, most of the council joined the table and one of them asked, "What about the trail to the upper levels?"

"I will explain that later."

"Also, several lodges will remain without anything inside and all the skins removed and sent to Calgary to be sold at the Trading Post. You did not see the corral, Chief Dalton. It has been taken down and only a small one has been built until we are finished. The posts and logs have been taken to the upper levels where men are building a barn and corral for the dog warrior horses.

"How long will it take to tear down the Great Hall and clean the lumber," Dalton asked.

"We will have over one hundred working and it will be done in three days," Benjamin continued. "Tomorrow, the big barn comes down and it will be ready for the wagons in one day."

Dalton spoke. "I noticed that half of our wagons are loaded with people. Everyone leaving is under fifty and can all ride. Only two wagons are needed for a mother and those children who cannot ride double on a horse.

Tomorrow, horses will be saddled and the riders will follow the wagons. The drivers will bring the horses back to the village and on the next morning we will saddle fresh horses for the trip.

I am concerned about the Police finding this village before we are finished. The trail from the Gordon Strong Ranch is starting to look more like a road. The Police are busy with drifters, Yankees and, yes, drunken Indians causing trouble in Lethbridge. It concerns me that something may cause them to look for someone and if they see this road turning south to the mountains, they will follow it."

Everyone agreed and Dalton asked Benjamin to continue.

"Now, the water culverts to the two pools have been closed. We have plugged them with solid cedar and greased the openings. Canvass has been placed over the ends and hollow cedar cappings placed over the canvass and greased. They do not leak. The same will be done with the water lines and culverts in the Great Hall when it is torn down.

Do you remember on the upper level where the hot water came out from a ledge, flowed a short distance and disappeared into another ledge?"

They all nodded.

"In the morning, I will take five stonebreakers to the upper levels and fill in the trench that leads to the large culvert that brings the hot water down to the village. We will do stonework to cover the mouth of the culvert in order to keep the culvert clean and to keep out small animals.

The only culverts and hot water lines left will be those used for the young warriors' village. I hope the dog warriors enjoy the hot pools while we are on the plains freezing."

Dalton and the dog warriors had a good laugh.

"Do you need any more buildings?" Benjamin asked.

Wandering Buffalo spoke. "There will be only two hundred or so of us left. The small Great Hall with the pool inside is big enough. There is a room for the women and the men and there is food storage going into a cave behind the kitchen. We could ask no more."

"Now, someone asked about the trail to the upper levels. When the Great Hall has been taken down, me and the stonebreakers will put small charges of dynamite above the Great Hall and about a mile above the trail. The charge will bring down dirt, rock and trees. When it is over, the Great Hall and the trail never existed.

Also, we will use the dirt to fill in the pools. We will plant trees along the edge and bring dead leaves to spread everywhere. It will look like the trees have been there for a long while. We will do the same with all the trails, especially the one that leads to the cleared land where the gardens and woodpiles are located."

"Why are we capping the ends of the water lines and culverts?"

"Who knows! Maybe in a year or two we will come back and buy this land."

There was laughter and shoulder hugs for Benjamin and his stonebreakers.

"Within ten days, all these things will be done. We will start moving the dog warrior teepees and lodges to the upper levels first thing in the morning while the trail is still open. After relocating on the upper levels, the dog warriors will take a new trail to hook up with the north trail that leads to the Gordon Stone Ranch. The road from the ranch to Lethbridge is just a normal road and will not cause anyone to ask questions.

The meeting broke up just as the sun began to dip over a mountain top. Dalton asked the council to meet in the morning to discuss the money.

After a good night's sleep, Dalton had a big breakfast and headed to the Wandering Buffalo Lodge. Beth and her young assistants were waiting. Dalton sat down at the long table and a young assistant gave a report on the money.

"I will read this page."

Money in banks to keep accounts opened	200.00
Cash on hand	39,000.00
Credit with Landsdown	17,000.00
Total cash and credits	$56,200.00

"How much money will we need?"

"We will need sixty to sixty-five thousand dollars to get everyone out of the village.

"So we are coming up about ten thousand dollars short?" Dalton asked.

"Not really. Do not forget that the money it will cost includes payment for personal items, horses left behind and wagons. Now, we do not know what the items going to the Trading Post will show us. The wagons and horses will be taken to the Gordon Stone Ranch and sold for good money. Also, there will be about fifty more wagon loads of product for Landsdown. We are not worried about Landsdown. Vincent tells us that so far as Landsdown is concerned, there might just be a credit."

"If I had to guess, I would say that the nation will have a few thousand dollars when we are finished."

Everyone showed appreciation for the work done by the young assistants.

"How many of our people have left the village?" Raincloud asked.

"About three hundred have left and fifty or more are leaving every day," Wandering Buffalo said.

"So in about seven or ten days, only the dog warriors will be left. Is that correct?" Raincloud asked.

"Yes. Ten days at the most," Wandering Buffalo replied.

"That will be just about right. In ten days we will make plans for the McAllister visit," Dalton stated.

"Anything from Anne and the kids?" Beth asked.

"Yes. They will be at the McAllister settlement tomorrow."

"I will pray for them."

"Pray for McAllister," Dalton said.

When the meeting was over, Raincloud and Dalton went to meet the stonebreakers.

"When you are done here, I want you to show three or four of the dog warriors how the dynamite works," Dalton stated.

"I will pick four to help bring down the side of the mountain. It will be a good start for them," Benjamin said.

As Dalton turned around, one of the groomers sent to the Ranch approached Dalton and Raincloud.

"Gordon has sent me, Chief Dalton. One of the drivers stopped at the ranch this morning and told us that you are concerned about the trail that has now become a road."

"Yes," Dalton said.

"Gordon has a plough and enough teams for two more ploughs. If you send two ploughs and four workers, we will begin ploughing a quarter mile on both sides of the road right up to the turn-off into the ranch.

When you are done with the wagons, we will then plough the road. Gordon said he will buy the ploughs or give them back to you when we are done. We will plant potatoes and corn in the spring."

"You tell Gordon that if he does this for us, he can have the ploughs. You keep saying 'we'."

"Yes. I will marry Theresa soon and you are all invited."

Dalton and Raincloud gave the young groomer shoulder hugs and assured him they would be there.

"What is your new name?" Raincloud asked.

"I am Samuel McLeod."

"Well, Sam, you tell Gordon the ploughs will be dropped off in the morning," Dalton stated.

Dalton and Raincloud watched Samuel ride north.

"A groomer one day, a husband the next," Dalton said.

"Our hired help is getting less every day. We should have a fence built from the corral down to the lower level so our horses do not drop off the steep side," Raincloud said.

"I am glad you mentioned it. When they get chasing around, they could very well take a fall, especially the new born. With the mountains on one side and the corral built across the top, it will not take long to put the fence up.

Tomorrow I will leave for Cut Bank. Anne and the kids are going to meet me there and I will stay in Cut Bank until they get the information we need. It is a two-day ride to Cut Bank so if everything works out, the four of us should be back in about seven days. I put you in charge of the fence!"

"Thanks!"

The two laughed as they walked.

It was July twenty-ninth, eighteen eighty-nine and twenty-four days since the massacre.

Chapter Twelve

The McAllister Settlement

"You are going to have to get those boots off, Cowboy."

Dalton left the village at sunrise and stopped at a Flathead camp to say Hello. He wanted to know if they heard of McAllister.

"Have you done any business in a settlement by the name of McAllister?" Dalton asked their chief.

"Once but that is all."

"I take it that you do not care for McAllister that much."

"McAllister says one thing and does another. We took him a small amount of gold and he cheated us on the price. When we saw the weight, he gave us less money than what it was worth. We know this because in Cut Bank, they pay more.

When we told him, he said the price of gold went down. We travelled too far so we took the money."

"Yes. He is not the kind of man you want to do business with. Does he ever go to Cut Bank?"

"No. A little while ago, he thought the railroad would go through his land but the railroad people decided to put it north in Cut Bank. They say he went there to buy land but the rich men from the east who follow the railroad got there before him.

He is not liked by the railroad people and they will not even sell him land for more. He is not wanted in Cut Bank."

"Good! Because that is where I am going.

Me and my friends will soon pay McAllister a visit. We will have many horses and cattle to take to our village. If you give us twenty riders and let us go through your land, we will give you half."

"We have rifles but not much bullets."

"I will make sure you have bullets. Your part is not to kill anyone but it does not hurt to have bullets. I want your riders to round up the livestock and herd them here through your land. There will be a few riders from our nation who will know when to start rounding up the cattle and horses."

"When will this happen?"

"In about fifteen days."

"We will be ready!"

Dalton nodded and rode east to Cut Bank.

The next morning, Dalton reached a high place overlooking Cut Bank. He took his glasses from the saddle bag and looked around. The town was crowded with railroad people and a work camp was set up on the south side.

He took his time and reached the livery in less than an hour.

"Is there a good place to stay?" Dalton asked.

"Quiet or rowdy?"

"I am expecting my family so I guess a quiet place with meals is what I am looking for," Dalton replied.

The livery owner pointed to a large boarding house almost the size of the one in Calgary.

"How much do you need for my horse?"

"Two dollars a day including feed."

"I think I will be here for about three days. If anyone asks for me, tell them where I am. Joseph is my name."

Dalton gave the livery owner six dollars and left for the boarding house. He paid for a spacious room and went upstairs to clean up.

After a short lie down, Dalton left the boarding house to look the town over.

It was day two since the McLeod family reached the settlement. Just before noon, McAllister walked down the planks to greet the McLeod family.

"How did you enjoy your rooms, Mrs. McLeod?" McAllister asked.

"The rooms were very nice. I sure wish you would let us pay for them," Anne replied.

"Nonsense! We will not need the rooms until tomorrow. On Fridays and Saturdays, we get company from Fort Benton and a few of the neighboring settlements. Our cowhands like to come in from the ranches and blow off a little steam. Not to worry though! You and Sarah can have my guest room. It is very nicely decorated and I can assure you that it will be very exclusive."

"That would be asking too much."

"Not at all! I insist! There is also room at the ranch for your son."

McAllister was looking at Sarah just about all the time he was talking.

"That will not be necessary, Mr. McAllister. Mother and I are riding out this afternoon to look at a couple of those abandoned ranches. The maps you gave us is all we will need. We have buffalo robes and supplies for two days and should return on Sunday," Michael said.

"Then why not move Sarah and your mother into the guest room right now?"

"I would feel a lot better if we did. I do not like the idea of Sarah sleeping above a saloon," Anne stated.

"Fine! You folks bring in your luggage and I will have the saloon bring us over some dinner."

McAllister could not take his eyes off Sarah as she walked down the planks and took the stairs to the rooms above the saloon.

"This is the son of a bitch who killed your brother and my son! I have to get away or shoot him!"

"I feel the same way. I could shoot him while you and Michael killed the four deputies. It would take less than a minute to kill them. All they do is sit around a table and play cards."

"We have to settle down. The maps he gave us locating the land he owns is one piece of the information we were after," Michael stated.

"You are right, Michael," Anne continued. "Sarah, you have today, Friday and Saturday to find out about the money, titles and fire power. Are you ready to get the information?"

"I will get the information!"

"Good. Me and Michael will leave right after lunch and meet you Sunday before noon."

The three moved their luggage to the guest room and after lunch, Michael and Anne rode northwest.

"That was a fine dinner, Mr. McAllister. I will heat some water and clean up these dishes."

"You will do no such thing. We will gather them up and let the saloon wash them."

They gathered up the dishes and took them through the door leading to the saloon. After placing them on the shelves in the hallway, McAllister offered Sarah a drink.

"Now that mother is gone, I think a small drink would be fine."

McAllister walked to his private bar and returned with a fancy bottle along with two small glasses. He filled the glasses almost to the brim and raised his glass to Sarah.

"Here is to you and your marvelous family."

McAllister took his drink down in one swallow. Sarah took a sip and held her throat doing a good job of pretending it was her first drink. McAllister poured himself another drink.

"I take it your mother does not approve of drinking?"

"My father did enough drinking for the whole family."

"Did?"

"Yes. My father is dead. After drinking most of the afternoon, he left the hotel and was run over by a wagon loaded with hides. The front wheel crushed his chest." Sarah lowered her head as she spoke.

"I am sorry to hear about your father. Where are you folks from?"

"Winnipeg," Sarah replied.

"Ah yes, Winnipeg -- the gateway to the west for your country. Was your father a rancher?"

"No. My father imported textiles. We had a nice store and warehouse in a small town near Winnipeg."

"What brings you to this end of the world?" McAllister asked.

"End of the world is right. I did not want to come but mother did not want to start out alone. I guess you might call it a new start for us. My mother was a rancher's daughter, Mr. McAllister."

"I see. So it is back to the roots. Well, my wife left for the east two years ago and my daughter married a wealthy rancher east on the Missouri. The west is too rough for some people.

I have a beautiful ranch house just over the bridge about a half hour from here. Would you like to take a ride out and look it over?"

"Yes. It would help pass the time."

"I will bring your horse from the livery and meet you back here in fifteen or so."

When McAllister returned, Sarah was on the planks and the two rode west over a wooden bridge that spanned a small creek.

"Does that creek overflow into the settlement in the spring?" Sarah asked.

"Not anymore. We built a small dam upstream to hold back the water. In the fall, we will let the water out to get ready for the spring runoff."

After crossing the bridge, McAllister pointed to a huge ranch house near the top of a high place. The two turned their horses south and rode for the ranch.

"Do you have a fella waiting for you back home?"

"No. I had a boyfriend about my age but somehow he forgot to grow up. I knew him quite well, if you know what I mean. My mother did not like him. She actually said he was too young for me."

"How old are you?"

"I am twenty-one, Mr. McAllister"

"Call me Bill."

"How old are you, Bill?"

"I am fifty-one years old."

"Well, you certainly do not look that old."

McAllister smiled and thanked Sarah for the compliment. When they reached the ranch house, an elderly Chinese hired hand came from the corral and led the horses to the barn. McAllister held the door as they stepped into the house.

"This place is huge!"

"Yes, I guess we had big ideas."

McAllister showed Sarah every room and made a special point of showing Sarah several closets filled with women's clothing.

"I think the clothes in my daughter's room will fit you quite well. Why don't you pick out a couple of outfits for Friday and Saturday. I will watch from the bar while you model them for me."

"Are you sure?"

"I am positive."

McAllister went downstairs to the bar and waited for Sarah to appear on the balcony.

After a few minutes, Sarah walked out on the balcony wearing a long black outfit that fit her perfectly. She walked back and forth to cheers from McAllister. The cheers were even louder when she returned to the balcony with a burgundy outfit.

"I hope you do not mind me borrowing the jewelry and shoes for the occasion?"

"They are yours! Put them in a bag with the dresses and come down for a drink."

"Bring your drink up! I think I will have a problem with the zipper on this dress. You can bring a drink for me if it is not too strong."

McAllister opened his mouth and took a deep breath. He downed his drink and took two bottles and two glasses from the bar. He could almost hear his heart beating as he walked up the stairs to the bedroom.

McAllister put the glasses and bottles down and walked over to where Sarah was standing. She raised both arms as McAllister reached behind to pull down the zipper. He was shaking but managed to get the zipper half down as she unbuttoned his shirt. Sarah reached behind and pulled the zipper all the way down as the dress slipped over her shoulders and onto the floor.

"You are going to have to get those boots off, Cowboy."

McAllister was speechless as he struggled with his boots and pants. Sarah slipped in between the covers and McAllister moved in beside her. She spread her legs and McAllister went into her with great pleasure.

When it was over, McAllister rolled over and told Sarah she was the greatest woman he had ever met.

"Well, great women get hungry, Bill."

"Yes! Of course! I will light a fire and put some water on the stove. The master bedroom has a tub, a pump and everything a woman needs. I will use the bath downstairs and make us something to eat."

"Do not make too much. You have to show me the other two bedrooms."

McAllister laughed and assured her it would be his pleasure to show her the other two bedrooms.

Sarah got out of bed and took a big swig from the bottle of whiskey.

"Ah! This is more like it!"

She took the small bottle and a glass into the master bedroom and after pouring herself a sweet drink, she went into the bathroom.

"Jesus! Everything a woman needs is right! This bathroom is bigger than most bedrooms!"

Sarah pumped water into the huge bathtub and felt the water. It was lukewarm as the water came from exposed pipes. She took the pail from the stove and poured the heated water into the tub. She felt the water and it was on the hot side which she liked. She filled up the pail with cold water and put it back on the stove.

When she returned to the bathroom with a full glass of sweet whiskey, Sarah examined the many bottles. One of them had bubbles written on it so she poured half into the tub and splashed the water. Bubbles appeared immediately. She left the half full bottle within reach and with glass in hand, she stretched out in the tub. Every time she moved, the bubbles increased until only her head was visible.

After a good soak, Sarah got out of the tub and opened the door to the bathroom closet. She found a towel and as she unfolded it, the towel was almost the size of a small blanket.

"Jesus! How big was that woman!"

McAllister yelled up that supper was ready and Sarah was a little relieved for she was getting drunk. She saw another bottle that had a rubber ball sticking out of the top and gave it a squeeze. The misty smell was just amazing.

"Why not!"

Sarah walked downstairs with one hand on the railing and the other hand holding a full glass of sweet whiskey. All she had on was a huge towel tied at the top and a belt around the waist.

McAllister laughed and called her Cleopatra.

"We have a cut of steak that few people understand. I hope you like the silver dollar fried potatoes and beets."

"Yes. I love Piapot beets!"

"Piapot beets?"

"Oh, it is just a saying from the Red River. This cut of steak is absolutely delicious, Bill! Where do you get it?"

"Now take a look at this 'T' bone steak. Do you see this round part on one side?"

Sarah nodded.

"I cut away two of these pieces and that is what you are eating. Two of the best cuts of steak in the entire world!"

"The sauce you put on top of them really makes the meal!" Sarah exclaimed.

"Yes. We have Ben and his wife to thank for the sauce. The Chinese know more about sauce than anyone I ever met."

"Where did you find the Chinese?"

"I stole them from the railroad."

They both had a good laugh and continued asking questions.

"You know, my mother left me two hundred dollars to put in your bank. Being practically in the middle of nowhere, are you not concerned about drifters coming by and robbing your bank?"

"I am not concerned at all. I have four deputies posted at all times, and my ranch hands to the west and to the east are on the lookout for drifters and will hunt anybody down who steals a blade of grass on my land."

"I do not think my mother is that worried about two hundred dollars but she will be bringing a lot more when we move west. Do your ranch hands know how dangerous it is out here?"

"Well, some are ranch hands and some are gunfighters."

"Why do you have gunfighters herding cattle?"

"Let me tell you something. About a month ago, five Indians came down from the north to deliver some wagons and wood. We cut a deal for twelve hundred dollars, a few days before, with some kind of half breed who spoke English very well. Anyhow, when they showed up, two of my deputies took them to the bank to pay them their money. Once inside the bank, they pulled guns on my deputies and took not only their twelve hundred dollars, but all the money in the bank."

"How much did they take?"

"They took five hundred dollars. However, my deputies rode out after them and somewhere to the north, this side of what the Flatheads call the Snake River, my deputies cornered the rotten thieves and killed them all. We got our money back so do not worry about drifters.

The gunfighters are here because we thought there might be trouble."

"I am less worried now than I was before."

"Good!"

"Tell me, Bill, why do you only have five hundred dollars in your bank? That is not very much money for a bank."

"I will show you something when we get back to town tomorrow." McAllister had a smile on his face when he said it and Sarah was glad they were there for the night.

McAllister got up and poured himself another drink while Sarah sipped from her glass.

"How did you end up with so many ranches?"

"I will tell you tomorrow when the saloon closes. I will not have much time to spend with you during the day but we will sure have a good time when six o'clock rolls around. I have a reserved table for a few guests and I am anxious to show you off. Wear that black outfit!"

Sarah thought this would be a good time to stop asking questions. She got up and went to where McAllister was sitting and as he turned to face her, she sat on his leg and untied the top of the towel which fell over her shoulders. McAllister kissed her gorgeous breasts.

"I think it is time to take a look at those other two bedrooms, Bill."

"Yes! And can I ask you to do what you did the first time?" McAllister asked.

"Of course. What we do is our business. I do not want my mother and brother to ever hear about this. I am not a Friday night whore, Bill."

"Of course," Bill whispered.

The two made their way upstairs to use the other two bedrooms.

Chapter Thirteen

"Bang! Bang!"

"The next time I will put the Sioux death hold on you!"

Shortly after seven o'clock, Michael and Anne reached a high place and could see in the distance, the abandoned ranch that was on their map. Michael took the glasses from a saddle bag and took a long look.

"This is perfect!" Michael exclaimed.

He handed the glasses to Anne and after looking things over, she agreed.

"Chief Dalton is going to like the location of this ranch. It is close to the Flathead nation and McAllister's ranches are just over those hills to the south" Michael pointed out.

"Is this where the Flatheads will gather to help herd the cattle?"

"Yes. I am sure Chief Dalton will approve of this location." Michael continued, "There is a nice little stream down there. Do you want to camp here for the night or shall we keep going?"

"No. Let us camp here."

Good! You go down by the stream and find a nice place while I double back to where we saw those rabbits."

Anne rode down and found a grassy spot near the stream. After watering, she took the saddle and bridal off her horse and tied him to a tree. As Anne began setting up camp, she heard a shot and smiled.

"Rabbit! I just love rabbit!"

She walked a short distance to the stream and put her hand in the water. With Michael not in sight, she took a large doe skin from her bedroll and removed her clothes.

She left the doe skin along with her clothes on a large flat rock and waded into the water up to her waist. She dived forward, swam on her back and dunked several times. Not wanting to be caught, she soon headed for the flat stone.

Michael reached the top of the hill in time to see Anne step out of the water and take the doe skin from the rock. He took his horse behind the small brush and watched her dry off.

"Jesus! I can see where Sarah got her great body!" Michael whispered.

Michael waited until Anne got her clothes on before he appeared at the top of the hill. Anne was placing jars of berries on the flat rock as Michael rode down the slope.

"I will hobble the horses and let them graze while you take care of this rabbit."

"Supper!" Anne exclaimed.

When Michael returned, Anne had the rabbit cleaned and ready for roasting. Michael started a fire while Anne secured the rabbit with a steel rod.

Michael placed large stones on either side of the small fire as a cradle for the steel rod. Anne brought the rabbit and placed it over the fire. They both laughed and turned the rabbit over the fire telling each other how much they both loved rabbit.

During supper, Michael brought up the question of Sarah and McAllister.

"Do you think Sarah will be safe with that rotten son of a bitch?" Michael asked.

"The way he was almost drooling over her, I think she will be just fine."

"I went along with leaving her behind because you did not seem too worried. Are you sure we should not go back?"

"We do not have to go back. Would you like to hear a little story?"

Michael smiled. "I like little stories. Go ahead."

"A few months ago, me and Big Man Walking rode to the Gordon Stone Ranch to visit with Gordon and Heather. Her sister Helen from Calgary was there and after supper, when we were alone outside, she thought it was her duty to tell me about Sarah."

Anne went on to tell Michael about Landsdown, the rich bankers and the killings.

"This is almost too much to believe! What did Big Man have to say when you told him?"

"Big Man does not know and neither does anybody else in the village except your father."

"What about Gordon and Heather? They are people of the cross now."

"They know about Sarah killing Cathy but they do not know about the rest. Helen said it was only for me to know."

"Why did you not tell Big Man? He is the father after all."

Anne smiled and cut a leg from the rabbit. Michael watched as she took a spoonful of berries from the jar after each bite.

"Michael, this is so delicious!"

"Well! Well! Why did you not tell Big Man?"

Anne was clearly amused.

"You really do like little stories! Let me tell you why.

At first, I was angry and disappointed. As you well know, Sarah is my only daughter and she is but nineteen years old. She will be twenty in August. Let me see now. Yes, August seventh matter of fact."

Michael gave Anne an annoyed look.

"Alright, let me continue. At a young age, my father was killed by the Sioux and we had to live with them. Later, the Blackfoot took us after one of their horse stealing raids and we were then forced to live with them. Then, when Chief Piapot came and slaughtered the Blackfoot, we had to live with the Assiniboine.

It was different this time. My mother asked Chief Piapot to take us with him. I was twelve years old and Chief Piapot sold us to Wandering Buffalo for one of his buffalo horses. I thought Wandering Buffalo was very handsome."

Michael rolled his eyes and looked towards the sky.

"Alright, I will continue. It did not matter if it was Sioux, Blackfoot or Assiniboine. The men were all alike. They took as many wives as they wanted and had fun with the young maidens while the women hauled wood, made food and raised children.

I know things are changing but not that much. Chief Three Killer made my mother a Chief and that shocked a lot of warriors. Chief Piapot allowed my mother to have a church within our nation and those of the cross who get married do not chase after women as they once did.

On the way home from the ranch, my anger became less. By the time Sarah showed up a few days ago, I was beginning to feel almost proud of her. She has opinions and I do not think men will use her as a toy.

The only man I know of in the nations who treats a woman with respect is Wandering Buffalo. He is the best stepfather and husband in this nation."

"So! You did not tell Big Man Walking about Sarah because Big Man has fun with other women. Is that correct?"

"Yes. What about you Michael? Do you have an eye for other women?"

"I am not of the cross."

"My God! I would think that you younger men would change!"

Anne rolled over behind Michael and put a headlock on him with her legs. She shook his head with great force.

"My ears! My ears!"

"Do you give?"

"I give! I give!"

Anne took her legs from around his head and pushed him away with both feet. Michael rolled twice ending up on his back. He laughed so hard he could not get up.

"Jesus, Anne! You are dangerous!"

"The next time, I will put a Sioux death hold on you!"

Michael rolled on the ground with laughter.

"You should take a swim before it gets dark. I will get the horses and tie them up for the night."

Michael agreed and headed for the stream.

After his swim, Michael hauled more wood and waited for Anne. In a few minutes, Anne appeared with the horses and tied them up. Michael spread the two robes near the fire and they sat down.

They went over the maps and agreed that in the morning, they would take a look at an abandoned ranch just a few hours southwest of their camp.

"Do you see these small hills to the south that run east and west?"

"Yes" Anne replied.

"Just over these hills, we can see McAllister's west ranch and livestock. We will go there after we stop at the abandoned ranch."

Anne nodded her head and looked over her shoulder to the east. Michael knew she was thinking about Sarah.

"Do you think McAllister will bang her?"

"Bang!?" Anne exclaimed.

"You know . . . . like you know."

"Yes, I know what you mean but could you not find a better word?"

"I picked it up at the Fort a little while ago. I kinda like it."

"Do you want me to put the Sioux death hold on you?"

"No! Not the Sioux death hold!" Michael exclaimed as he shook with laughter.

Anne laughed along with him.

When they settled down, Anne threw a log on the fire and turned to look at Michael.

"Yes. I think he will BANG her" Anne stated.

Michael just shook his head as he rolled up his saddle blanket and long rain coat for a pillow. Anne did the same and the two lay down on one side of their robe and pulled the other side over them.

It was getting dark out now but the fire gave them just enough light to see.

"I remember when you were born. I was fifteen years old. You must be almost thirty years old now."

"Yes. Twenty nine and you must be almost fifty now."

"You are asking for it! I am forty-four years old!"

Michael laughed and said to Anne, "Who would ever guess that you are so much fun."

"This is the first time in a long time that I have been alone with another man. Did you forget the little story I told you?"

"No."

"Tomorrow, after we find out what is over those hills, could we come back here and camp before we head out east to McAllister's other ranch? It is so beautiful here!"

"Sure. We will have lots of time to make it back here for the evening."

The two lay back on their pillows and tried to get some sleep. Michael rolled around and his mind began to wander. After an hour or so, Michael asked Anne if she was awake.

"I am deep in sleep" Anne replied.

"I am cold" Michael said in a whisper.

"Cold! My God! I am sweating!"

"Maybe I am getting a chill, like when you are getting sick."

"Well, we cannot have you getting sick what with all the riding we have to do tomorrow. Bring your robe and furry side down."

Anne threw back her robe and Michael spread his robe over Anne with the furry side down. He was about to crawl in when Anne stopped him.

"Boots!"

"Oh! Yes!"

Michael managed to get his boots off even though he was a little shaky.

"I guess you know that those riding pants are not really the smoothest thing on a girl's skin."

Michael removed his riding pants and crawled in between the furry robes. Anne sat up and removed her blouse. She got back down between the covers and moved over next to Michael. He put his arms around her shoulder as Anne spread her legs. Michael moved in between Anne's legs and banged her until sweat poured down her face.

"How is the chill?"

"You are so beautiful" Michael whispered.

They spoke for a while and held each other close.

Chapter Fourteen

The West Ranch

"Then you will be of the cross and go to church?"

In the morning, Anne reached over to touch Michael but he was not there. She looked around and saw him standing waist deep in the water motioning her to join him. Anne smiled and waded out to where Michael met her with open arms.

They splashed around and walked hand in hand to the shore.

"Should we use the robes before we get riding?" Michael asked.

Anne looked down between Michael's legs.

"Yes, I think we should. If we stay on top, the skins will dry us off."

When they finished rolling around on the skin, Michael left to saddle the horses while Anne lit a fire and heated the smoked strips of beef. Michael soon returned and kissed Anne on the neck.

After their breakfast of beef and berries, they began to gather up the supplies.

"We should leave everything here. We are coming back for the evening" Michael said.

"Good idea! We should take the robes with us though just in case you get another chill."

They both had a good laugh and broke camp.

It did not take long to reach the abandoned farm house. Michael dismounted and walked to the planks. The door was open. Anne tied the horses and they went inside.

"Jesus! This place is in better shape than I thought" Michael exclaimed.

"Look at the huge fireplace! And there is a pump in the kitchen!"

"Whoever had this place must have been in a hurry to leave. They did not even take the stove or table and chairs" Michael added.

They even left the beds!" Anne continued. "All this place needs is a good cleaning. What about the ceiling?"

"The ceiling is good. If it leaked, it would show up on the walls or the floor. Let us take a look at the barn and corral" Michael added.

The two took a good look around and found just a few repairs needed for the barn and corral.

"Everything is just fine. If the pumps work, this place is ready for a family" Michael said.

"I saw a pail in the kitchen" Anne continued. "I will go get it and we can try the outside pump first."

Anne returned with a pail and they went to the nearby stream to get water for priming. It did not take long before they got both pumps working.

Michel and Anne looked at each other as they stood in the middle of the room. Michael knew what Anne was thinking.

"We will talk about it tonight" Michael said with a smile.

It took less than two hours to reach the small hills that ran east and west. They removed everything from the horses and Michael put on the hobbles. When they neared the top, they crawled to a high place and Michael looked through the glasses.

After taking a good look, he turned to Anne and said nothing. His eyes were wide and his mouth was open as he handed the glasses to Anne. She looked through the glasses and turned to Michael with the same amazed look.

"My God! There must be over a thousand cattle out there!" she exclaimed.

"They are spread out along the plains like when the buffalo were here. There are hundreds of horses too." Michael continued, "My father is not going to believe this! It will take a hell of a lot more than twenty riders to bring this herd in!"

"I wonder where he got them all?"

"He stole them. That is why the ranches are abandoned."

Michael and Anne walked to a higher place to observe the gunfighters ranch house. Michael looked at the map and everything was where it was supposed to be.

"Well, we can head back. We have seen what we came to see" Michael said.

"I think we should let the horses graze for a while. We have our robes."

"Good idea. I feel a chill coming on."

It was just a little before four o'clock when Michael and Anne rode back to their camp. Michael hobbled the horses while Anne got a fire going.

"There are so many fish in that stream I think I could catch one with my hands" Michael said.

"I think you had better use the hook."

Michael cut a length from a rope and unbraided it. He tied the small pieces together so that it was about twenty feet long. He then cut a small straight tree, cleaned the branches and tied the rope to the tree in several places. He left about two feet near the end dangle in the water. After securing the hook and putting on a little bait, he let the small tree float downstream.

Anne sat on a flat rock and watched. Michael soon got a bite and pulled the rope. Anne jumped up and down as Michael reached in the water and showed her a good sized fish.

"I will gather up some fresh berries while you clean the fish."

Anne left with a small jar and returned with fresh berries and a very large leaf.

"Where did you find the leaf?"

"I found it floating underneath the water."

Michael put the fish over the fire as Anne sprinkled it with salt, pepper and the leaf that she cut into tiny pieces.

"God! Does this ever smell good!" Michael exclaimed.

Anne removed the hot pan from the fire and placed it on a flat rock. She poured the berries over top and gave Michael a fork. His eyes lit up as he forked down the fish. When they were almost full, Michael leaned over and gave Anne a kiss.

"The best, Anne! The very best!"

After cleaning up the camp, they sat on a flat rock and discussed their situation.

"So, what about you Michael? Have you got a woman?"

"Kinda."

"Kinda?" Anne asked.

"Well, the woman I am with now wants to live on the reserve and I do not. My father wants me to live in one of the towns and become a part of the white community.

This is not the only reason I do not want to stay with her. She is younger and without any skills. She does not even want to work in the garden or help out in the kitchen.

I have told her that I do not wish to get married. She has made friends with the younger people who live in the shacks and I do not wish to spend any more time with her. I wish to spend time with you."

"I wish to spend time with you too, but my situation is not quite as simple as yours. Maybe it is more simple than I think. My mother and Wandering Buffalo have told me several times to make a new start. Even Sarah does not approve of what her father is doing.

Big Man is spending more and more time with a young maiden. She is one of Chief Three Killer's granddaughters. Big Man wishes to move to Calgary but I want to stay here in the foot hills close to the mountains. When I told him, he did not have anything to say. I think he would be only too happy to move to Calgary with Chief Three Killer's granddaughter.

When I was twelve, I remember Chief Piapot telling my mother that the nation was not a prison and we could leave at any time. Chief Three Killer told us the same thing but my mother would never leave the mountains and Wandering Buffalo.

Your father would not allow anyone to stop me from going anywhere. So I guess we have to make a decision, Michael."

"When we walked through that abandoned farm house, I had you on my mind. Stay here. I am going to get the map."

Michael went to the saddle bags and returned with the map.

"This ranch land goes across the Milk River to the Canadian border."

"Milk River?"

"The Snake is now what the Yankees call the Milk River" Michael continued. "The ranch is just a few hours from the village. In the summer, a person could ride to the village for a visit and be back before sundown."

"This is just where I would like to live!"

"Do you wish to marry me Michael?"

"But you are already married. Your papers say Walker."

"I have not sent them yet. My name is McLeod."

"Why have you not sent them?"

"I was not sure. I thought about leaving."

Michael got up from the flat rock and pulled Anne to him.

"There is not another woman I would sooner marry" Michael continued. "Of course I will marry you!"

"Then you will be of the cross and go to church?"

"Yes."

"McAllister says this is only one of seven ranches he has available. I wonder what name the titles are registered under" Anne mused.

"This we will find out Sunday morning. If, for any reason, we cannot purchase this ranch, we can buy some land north of the Milk River in Canada" Michael stated.

"That would be just fine. The only difference is that this ranch has a house and barn" Anne said.

"Remember, north of the Milk River puts us even closer to the village."

Anne nodded and gave Michael a hug.

They both cleaned up the camp and spread their robes. After a quick swim, they decided to walk upstream just to look around before it got dark.

"We will get an early start tomorrow and ride east of the McAllister settlement" Michael continued. "We have to locate the other ranch and the rest of McAllister's gunfighters."

Anne nodded and they continued to talk as they walked.

Chapter Fifteen

Sarah Strikes Gold

"Oh my God! Is that gold?"

A little after six o'clock, Sarah heard a door open and shut as she stood in front of a mirror getting ready for the night. Sarah appeared on the balcony wearing the black outfit and had a string of pearls around her neck. McAllister gave Sarah a loud cheer and motioned her downstairs.

McAllister went to his private bar and poured two drinks of whiskey.

"If you want to live in the west, you have to take the odd drink of whiskey."

"Could I just shoot it back and take a sweet drink?"

"Of course!"

Sarah shot her whiskey back and began to cough. McAllister poured her a sweet drink which Sarah shot back as well.

"Ah! That's better! My throat was burning."

"More whiskey?" Bill asked.

"Maybe a glass of whiskey and a glass of liqueur or whatever you call it. I will just sip on both of them."

"That sounds like a good idea."

Bill brought the two bottles over to the table and filled the glasses.

"Yesterday, I told you that I would tell you why there was only five hundred dollars in the bank. Well, that locked door over there leads to the saloon. At the end of the hallway is another locked door before you enter the saloon. This you already know.

Now over here we have the same thing only this door leads to the bank. Bring your drink. I want to show you something."

Sarah brought her drink and followed McAllister into the bank hallway. Halfway down the hall, McAllister moved a picture from the wall and lifted some kind of catch. A large door made of the same vertical wooden paneling as the wall opened just a crack. McAllister pulled the wooden door open wide and looked at Sarah.

"My God! What a beautiful steel door! What is that shiny round dial?"

"This is the combination lock. You have to know the numbers to open it. I bought the door in the east and the railroad Police delivered it in the evening. The Police brought two workers from the east and the six of us pushed it up rollers an inch at a time. It took us until morning but we got it done.

The frame is made of steel set into concrete which also has steel."

McAllister unlocked the steel door and after lighting the lamps, he motioned for Sarah to come inside. Sarah walked in and could not believe what she saw. Steel shelves were stacked with paper money and gold bricks were stacked on the floor off to one side.

"Oh my God! Is that gold?"

"Solid gold my dear."

"How did you come by the gold bricks?"

"Every now and then, a banker from the east brings them to me, along with gold coins, in exchange for raw gold and paper. I pay him a little extra. The gold and silver coins are in those sacks beside the bricks."

"So this is why there is only five hundred dollars in the bank" Sarah stated.

"Yes. Now along this wall, just above the desk in those trays, is the paperwork for the ranches."

"Paperwork?" Sarah asked.

"Yes. The titles are still in the last owner's name but I have the paperwork necessary to foreclose and transfer whenever I want."

"Then why don't you?"

"If I get too many transfers to my name in a short period of time, who knows, maybe the feds will pay a visit. Not that I care but as you get older, you will learn to stay away from the feds. These people like to wave the flag and work for almost nothing. They are jealous of anyone with a dollar."

"I think I am learning right now and I agree with you" Sarah stated.

McAllister looked at his pocket watch.

"Good Lord! What about fire?" Sarah asked.

Bill smiled and removed a stack of money from a shelf. "Put your hand in there Sarah."

Sarah stuck her hand in and touched the wall.

"It is all steel!" she exclaimed.

Bill lifted a lamp and pointed at the ceiling. It was all steel panels and braced with short pieces of steel at forty-five degree angles.

"Is there concrete up there too?!"

"No. The steel is braced and the panels rest on top of the walls. Every square inch of this vault is lined with steel. The building could burn to the ground and nothing in this vault would be damaged.

Now, do you think your mother's money is safe in my bank?"

"Oh yes! Very much so!"

"Besides the railroad Police, we are the only two who know about this vault and I am the only one who knows the combination to the door. That is why the bank is only open on Friday and Saturday and I am the only employee."

"Why did you tell me?"

"I guess I want you to know that I can afford just about anything you may desire. When you get back from the east, I am hoping that our relationship could be a little more permanent."

Sarah smiled. "It is something to think about Bill."

Bill locked up the vault and they returned to the living room.

In just a few minutes, three very well-dressed, middle-aged men came to the door. Bill made the introductions and the five proceeded to the saloon. A young woman took them up two steps to a large table where three attractive ladies were already seated.

The table was set with the finest candles, dishes and tablecloth. Sarah pretended to be impressed for she had seen it all before. Once again, there were introductions all around.

A young Chinese worker approached the table and gave McAllister the three keys to the rooms he took the luggage for the guests. He disappeared up the private stairway that led to the rooms.

The saloon was packed with ranchers and those who followed the railroad. Everyone seemed to be enjoying themselves as they drank and danced to the music. There were several young girls working the floor.

Every now and then, a young girl would take the other stairs with one of the men. Two deputies sat near the stairs gambling with the guests. The bar was run by a middle-aged couple who also received food from the kitchen at one end of the bar.

A fight broke out between two cowboys and four deputies threw them out the door. Two cowboys wanted to go upstairs but the deputies told them to go outside and use the east stairway. There was some shoving but nothing came of it.

Sarah leaned over and said to Bill, "Who was that Chinese fella? He spoke pretty good English."

"Remember the old Chinaman that took our horses when we were at the ranch?"

Sarah nodded.

"That was his oldest son. On weekends, Tom and his wife take care of the rooms upstairs. His other son and daughter, along with her husband, work in the kitchen.

During the week, there is only Tom working in the kitchen. He made the dinner yesterday."

"Yes, and it was very good" Sarah stated.

After supper was served, one of the three women said to Sarah, "I understand you are from north of the border."

Sarah nodded.

"I didn't think you people cared that much for us."

"Well here I am. There is no reason for you to repeat rumors anymore. Now is there?"

The woman was clearly shaken by Sarah's aggressiveness and started a conversation with her dinner partner.

The other two women began speaking with Sarah and were a little more friendly. They were obviously afraid of getting the same treatment.

Bill had a slight smile as he listened to their conversation. He was impressed by the manner in which Sarah conducted herself.

During the evening, Sarah occasionally glanced at the open window to the kitchen and could see the three Chinese preparing food. Somehow, she had to speak with them. Everyone at the McAllister settlement had to be killed and she knew that Chief Piapot would not allow the killing of these Chinese people.

After supper, the McAllister group hit the dance floor. They had a good time dancing and requesting tunes. Just after midnight, the three guests and their women went to their rooms. Sarah and McAllister talked for a short while before retiring to their private quarters.

McAllister was full of compliments as they took the stairs to his bedroom.

In the morning, McAllister had to leave for the bank and told Sarah he would send Tom in with breakfast.

"I will go make breakfast for myself. It will give me something to do."

McAllister nodded and left for the bank.

After cleaning up, Sarah put on her slacks and went to the kitchen.

"Good morning Tom."

"Good morning Miss Sarah."

"Just call me Sarah. Bill tells me there are seven in your family."

"Yes, seven counting my wife and brother-in-law."

"How did you all end up here in this settlement?"

"We worked on the railroad but I guess Mr. McAllister paid the big boss some money and we were sent here to work for him."

"Does he pay you?"

"We do not pay anything for food or the bunkhouse. Clothing and everything else, we get from the store. Mr. McAllister keeps track and said he would deduct it from our pay when we leave."

"How much does he pay you?"

"We get seven dollars a day for all of us."

"When are you leaving?"

Tom looked at Sarah and then at the ground.

"So you do not know when you can leave" Sarah stated.

"I guess not. I wish we could leave tomorrow. It is like being locked up. I hope you do not tell anyone about this."

"Do not worry about that. Do you have papers?"

"No. We could not get any."

"Have you ever heard of Canada?"

"Yes. Some of our friends went that direction. They came once to Havre and we visited for a little while.

Our family wanted to go back with them but we were not allowed to leave. The people around here load and unload us like we are cattle."

"Have you ever heard of Calgary?"

"Yes. Our friends mentioned that place."

"Do they live in Calgary?"

"No. They have a small eating place east of Calgary."

"Now listen carefully Tom. Soon, within ten to fifteen days, riders will come to your bunkhouse in the middle of the night. Do not be afraid. We are going to take your family north to Canada. There is a man in Calgary who will arrange for all of you to get papers so you can go wherever you please."

"You can do all this?"

"Yes."

"Why?" Tom asked.

"The man I work for does not want you people killed" Sarah replied.

"You are going to kill McAllister!?"

"Yes, we are going to kill them all."

Tom smiled and said to Sarah, "Good!"

"Now you talk to your father and get ready to move out. How many wagons are there at the ranch?"

"There are two wagons outside and a covered wagon in the barn."

"Good! The women and your father can ride in the covered wagon and you will need a wagon for what you want to take with you. Do not worry about your money. We will have the money that McAllister owes you."

"Our father told us something good was going to happen" Tom said.

"What made him think something good was going to happen?"

"He said you were too beautiful for McAllister and you were not here for a good time."

Sarah smiled and said to Tom, "Tonight, when I look at you, nod if your family is ready."

"We will be ready!"

Sarah ate her breakfast and returned to the living quarters. She walked down the hallway and turned around with her back to the bank door. Sarah walked back down the hall taking long steps and stopped in front of the picture that marked the entrance to the vault.

"Four steps," she whispered.

She then went upstairs to the McAllister bedroom and did the same thing.

"The vault is right under the bed. Nothing like fuckin on top of a vault full of money," Sarah said in a whisper.

Sarah looked across the street at the livery and the adjoining store. There were rooms above the store where the deputies slept. Sarah walked across the street to the livery and met up with a deputy.

"So you do livery duty as well."

"Yes, only the deputies work in the livery and the store," the deputy stated.

"I just came to say Hello to my horse."

Sarah took a good look around as she walked out the back door to the corral. She stood on the other side of her horse so the deputy could not see her looking at the back of the store.

Before leaving, Sarah went into the store to look around. She took notice of a stairway that led to the rooms above the store. The door from the livery opened into the store just below the stairs. Sarah bought a piece of chocolate and walked back across the street into the saloon. McAllister's three friends were sitting at the big table eating breakfast.

"So what happened to the girls?" Sarah asked.

"They are taking turns soaking in the big tub," one of them replied.

"That sounds like a good idea."

Sarah left for McAllister's living quarters to soak in the tub and take a quick nap before getting ready for the Saturday night gathering.

Chapter Sixteen

Michael and Anne Make Plans

"I forgot you are a Yankee"

After riding since early morning, Michael and Anne reached a place just north of the McAllister settlement and south of Cut Bank.

"It is still a couple of hours before twelve o'clock. Now this is what we will do. You go north to Cut Bank and bring my father here to this place. I will ride east and take a look at the ranch where McAllister has his deputies posted. When I have taken a good look at everything, I will ride back here where the three of us will camp for the evening."

"That sounds good Michael but remember, three is too many."

"We will send him to the store" Michael stated.

The two had a good laugh and agreed that Dalton did not have to know about their plans. They leaned in their saddles for a quick embrace before Anne rode north and Michael rode east.

In less than an hour, Michael rode up a slope and tied his horse to a tree. He took his glasses and walked to the top of the slope overlooking two ranch houses. There were cattle grazing but not very many.

The ranch house to the southeast seemed to be abandoned with no sign of cattle, horses or deputies. The ranch house near the road east was anything but abandoned. There was a large corral with eleven horses and he could make out four deputies on the gun range shooting and drinking whiskey. Three deputies were on the planks eating as four deputies arrived from the settlement.

One of the four seemed to be in charge. He spoke to them for a short time before six deputies saddled up and headed for the settlement.

Michael observed the ranch house for an hour or two and went for his horse.

"It looks like eight at the ranch and probably four in the settlement" Michael said to himself.

Michael returned to the camp site just before three o'clock. Dalton and Anne were there already and had a fire going.

"We thought you got lost" Dalton exclaimed.

"I was not lost but I am hungry!"

"Well, you came to the right place! We picked up three steaks, onions, potatoes and a jar of Grandma's raspberries!" Anne exclaimed.

The three had a good laugh as Michael left to hobble his horse and put him out to graze.

When he returned, Dalton and Anne were busy cooking. Michael and Anne kept their distance and settled for a kind of 'I miss you' look. The steaks and potatoes were almost cooked as Dalton threw on the sliced onions. They all got even more hungry when the onions started to simmer in steak juice. Dalton and Anne filled their plates and Michael ate out of the fry pan.

"I guess we will need more riders to bring in the cattle and horses" Dalton said.

"Yes. That is why Anne went for you."

"I am going to leave for the Flathead nation right after we eat. The Flatheads will be pleased when I tell them the size of the herd. I was! They can probably give us a few more riders and we have more riders as well. I think we are going to need the Flatheads to help us hide the herd.

Now, tomorrow morning, pick up Sarah and ride to the village. I am going to send riders down this trail. If you are not at this place before two o'clock, we will come for you."

Michael nodded.

"We rode into the settlement from the east. How do we explain riding north?"

"Jesus, Anne! Let me eat!"

Michael and Anne laughed as Dalton tried to figure out an answer as he ate.

"Did Anne tell you about the ranch we saw? It is close to the border just below Lethbridge. We could buy the ranch and tell McAllister we are taking Sarah to see it before we catch a train from Lethbridge" Michael stated.

"You came from the east. How do you know about a train in Lethbridge?" Dalton asked.

"Jesus! Let me eat!" Michael shouted.

There was more laughter from Dalton and Anne. When they were done laughing, Dalton spoke. "I think I have the answer. When I bought the steaks from the butcher, I asked him where he got the fresh fish and ducks. He told me he paid the Flatheads for them. So just tell McAllister that you ran into these hunters and they told you about a town called Lethbridge where you could catch a train to the east."

Michael and Anne nodded.

"How much more money will you need to buy that ranch?" Dalton asked.

"We have close to three hundred dollars with the two hundred Sarah has deposited with McAllister. I think five hundred dollars should be enough" Anne stated.

"I think so too" Michael added.

Dalton went to his saddle bag and returned with three hundred in Yankee funds. Michael and Anne told Dalton they would take care of the camp. Dalton saddled his horse and rode west to the Flathead nation.

"This turned out pretty good."

"I will get the robes" Michael said.

After watering and hobbling the horses, Michael returned to camp with the robes. Anne was walking knee deep in water as he returned to camp.

"There is a nice sandy place just behind those rocks" Anne continued. "Bring the big skin and the small one. I need you to do my back."

Anne walked back and disappeared behind the big rocks. Michael returned with the skins and the white man's soap. Anne was sitting in the shallow water waiting to get her back washed. Michael joined her in the water and they took turns using the white man's soap.

After swimming and splashing around, Michael crawled to the edge of the stream and rested his head in the shallow water. Anne soon joined Michael and lay down beside him in the shallow water.

"This might be our last time alone for a few days" Michael said.

"Yes, I know. I have been thinking about that. Did you tell my father about us?"

"No. We agreed to leave it until after the massacre. Remember?"

There was laughter as Michael nodded his head and got a mouthful of water.

Anne rolled over and rested her left breast on Michael's chest. Michael kissed her neck and as she glanced down, she could see that Michael did not want to talk anymore.

"Have you ever been banged in the water, Michael?"

Michael shook his head.

"Guess what!" Anne exclaimed.

She moved on top of Michael and gave him a marvelous experience.

When it was over, they took a quick swim and after drying off, they returned to the camp. Michael got the fire going while Anne put the leftovers into the large pan and placed it over the fire. They both ate out of the large fry pan and shared spoonfuls of Grandma's raspberries.

"This is delicious! That workout made me hungry!" Anne exclaimed.

There was a brief silence as Michael looked at Anne.

"I love you Anne."

There was another moment of silence before Anne spoke.

"Sarah tells me that men often say that before but seldom say it after. I love you too Michael and we will do whatever it takes to be together."

Michael smiled and left to bring the horses in while Anne cleaned up the camp. When she was done, Anne went to meet Michael and they walked back together.

"Should we tell Sarah?" Michael asked.

"No. When we get back to the village, I will tell Big Man I do not want to live in Calgary. He might feel so strongly about going that maybe he will tell me he's going with or without me. Maybe that would be too much to ask but who knows?"

"On the other hand, he might want to spend all his time with another woman" Michael added.

"That would be good too" Anne stated.

The two continued walking and decided to just wait and see what happens. Michael took the horses to the stream for a last drink before tying them. Anne spread the robes and put a little more wood on the fire.

After Michael tied the horses, they got comfortable between the robes.

"It has been a long day" Anne said.

"Yes, and tomorrow will be the same" Michael stated.

"This is the third day for Sarah, I wonder how she is doing?" Anne pondered.

"Well, there is nothing we can do about it until morning but I will also be glad when she is out of there" Michael stated.

"How long do you think it will take us to reach the McAllister settlement?"

"Well, it took me about an hour to get above the east ranch and the settlement was just a little southwest. If we get up at sunrise, I am sure we can reach the settlement before ten o'clock. Well before noon, for sure.

Tell me about Big Man. I have not had much to do with him for years" Michael said.

"Big Man knows a great deal about healing and when he was made Chief of Medicine, he just could not handle the attention. Everyone looked up to him, especially young women, and he took advantage of the situation.

It is probably the only major thing wrong with him but so far as I am concerned, he has lost my respect and I cannot put it behind me."

"Then, with or without me, you are going to leave."

"Yes. I do not wish to sound like a little girl but I want to live close to my mother and Wandering Buffalo. Did you know that they are going to the little white church when this McAllister thing is finished?"

"No. Maybe we will go with them" Michael said.

"That would be so good! Just imagine, my mother and me getting married on the same day!"

"All put together, how much money do we have?" Michael asked.

"Well, with the money I will get from the nation and the money I was paid for working in the store, I probably have close to a hundred and fifty dollars. Big Man will get the money for the horses and other items. That is the way it works."

"The nation will give us enough money to buy one quarter of land. Also I have three horses in my father's herd. They are worth maybe two hundred dollars" Michael stated.

"Do you have any cash?" Anne asked.

"A year or so ago, I gave Vincent a hundred dollars to keep for me. He deposited my money in a Winnipeg bank. I told him to put it there so I would not spend it."

"So with my cash, your cash and horses we have four hundred and fifty dollars" Anne stated.

"Yes, and do not forget that we will get enough money to purchase one quarter of land" Michael added.

"Good Lord, we have enough to pay the nation for the ranch. If we can bargain McAllister down, maybe there will be money left over." Anne continued, "We should probably have Sarah make the deal!"

They both had a good laugh even though Anne was half serious.

"There is one other thing we are forgetting" Michael continued. "Whenever the nation goes to war, those up front get part of what is taken and the nation gets the rest."

"How much do you think we will get?" Anne asked.

"It will depend on how much is taken. Sarah will probably get more than us because she has put her life on the line. We have more or less been camping."

"And I have enjoyed every minute of it!" Anne exclaimed.

"Me too!" Michael added.

"Well, whatever we get from the nation, we should take more livestock than money" Anne suggested.

"I agree." Michael continued, "Because we have Canadian papers, will we have a problem buying land?"

"Land speculators are coming from all over the world to buy up land so I do not think it will be a problem. Anyhow, you are forgetting that I have Yankee papers.

According to people like Landsdown, you never give up your birth rights."

"I forgot that you are a Yankee" Michael said.

"Do you still want to marry me?"

"No. I hate Yankees."

Anne got to her knees and went for Michael's throat. Michael got one leg loose from under the robes. He raised his leg across Anne's chest and knocked her backwards and got to his feet. Anne came at him as Michael ducked down and threw her over his shoulder. He waded in the water and threw her in the stream.

Anne got up spitting water and ran towards Michael. He grabbed the big skin from the rock and headed up the slope towards the robes.

"I had to cool you off!"

"I will cool you off, you son of a bitch!"

"Wait! Wait! I am going to help dry!"

When Anne reached Michael, he moved to his left and wrapped the skin around her. Anne settled down as Michael started to dry her shoulders.

There was much laughter as they got back between the robes.

"I love you Michael."

"I love you too."

Chapter Seventeen

Sarah Closes the Deal

"I am going to miss you Mrs. McAllister."

Just before five o'clock, Sarah went to the bar and threw back some whiskey from the bottle. She poured McAllister a glass and gave herself a small shot of liqueur. McAllister soon arrived and Sarah gave him his drink.

"Good Lord! You look even better in that burgundy outfit than you did in the black one!" McAllister exclaimed.

Sarah smiled and did a few quick turns as Bill clapped and cheered.

"You do not know how nice it is to have such a beautiful woman who even knows enough to bring an old banker a drink after a hard day's work."

"Well, it is the least I can do for all the wonderful service I have been given."

The two sat at the table and talked about the weekend guests and how much fun they were having. Bill brought the two bottles to the table and filled up their glasses.

"Where did you find the couple that work the bar?"

"They have a small ranch near Havre. The woman used to work in a saloon and her husband followed the railroad before they bought the ranch. He heard about the settlement and asked me for a job. They come on weekends to pick up a few dollars and have some fun. They will leave first thing in the morning."

"Good! My mother and brother will probably be here before eleven o'clock. What about everybody else?"

"Everyone else will be gone except two deputies who will be asleep above the store. Sunday is Deputy Day if you know what I mean."

"Not exactly."

"Well, they make more money than those gunfighters out on the west range and they like the girls too. Early tomorrow morning, the girls will be taking the east road and they like to stop off for a while and visit with the deputies.

The only folks that are going to be around here at eleven o'clock Sunday morning are you and me, the two deputies and the Chinese."

"Could you get our guest room cleaned up first? I do not want my mother to know about us until I am ready to tell her."

"Of course. The Chinese will be cleaning all night. When they are done, your mother will never know how much we have been enjoying ourselves in those two rooms!"

Sarah laughed and gave Bill a kiss.

"Now what about us Sarah? I guess you know I love you and want you for my wife."

"Where would we live? I do not want to live beside a saloon and whores."

"We could build a house or live at the family ranch house."

"I love the ranch house and I love you Bill. My father left me some money. I could put some towards the ranch and be like a part owner!" Sarah exclaimed.

"Nonsense! If you marry me, I will put you on the title as half owner."

"Oh Bill, that would be so wonderful. I will tell mother before we get back from Winnipeg. She will be so happy!"

"Maybe she will not find anything she likes and not come back" Bill stated.

"She is coming back. Sell her the land and she will build if she has to."

"Your mother has money?"

"Yes."

"Look at the time! I am going to draw some water and have a quick bath. Too bad you are all dressed up. I could use a little something to get me through the evening."

"Go jump in the tub Bill. I will be along to give you a little something before you get dressed."

Bill smiled and took the stairs. He stopped at the top and told Sarah to give him fifteen minutes. Sarah smiled back and nodded.

Sarah threw back her liqueur and took a good belt of whiskey from the bottle. She waited a few minutes and took the stairs. The bedroom door was open and Bill was in his bathrobe. Sarah sat down on the end of the bed and motioned Bill over. As they came down the stairs, Sarah said to Bill, "We have to be up early in the morning."

"We will excuse ourselves before eleven o'clock" Bill said.

"Good. That will give us a little time to talk before we hit the bedroom" Sarah added.

The same six guests were at the big table when Bill and Sarah arrived. Much to Sarah's surprise, the girls were far more friendly this time.

"How the hell do you manage all this all by yourself? I could manage a bank but I don't know if I would have the patience to do all that accounting."

"Actually Jed, I am much like you. Accounting is something I refuse to do. The first Monday and Tuesday of each month an accountant and his wife come from Havre to take care of the accounting" McAllister stated.

"Well, here's to accountants" Jed said.

"I have a pleasant surprise for supper. Has anyone here had lobster tails?"

"Lobster tails!" one of the girls exclaimed.

The supper guests all shook their heads including Sarah. Sarah knew all about lobster tails and smiled as Bill went on about supper.

"After a bowl of special French soup, Tom and his wife will set the table for our lobster tail supper."

In a few minutes, Tom and his wife arrived at the table with two trays of soup. Tom reached around McAllister and placed his bowl of soup on the table. Sarah looked Tom in the eyes and he gave Sarah a nod. Sarah smiled and took a spoonful of soup.

"This soup is delicious!" one of the guests exclaimed.

"Yes. Pea soup. A specialty of the house" McAllister said.

There was laughter and compliments as the guests finished their bowls of soup.

Tom and his wife took the bowls away and returned to the table with eight small glasses of butter sitting in a holder with lit candles underneath to keep the butter hot. They returned to the kitchen and came back with the eight plates of hot food. Each plate had a lobster tail, a round filet of steak, roasted small potatoes and two kinds of vegetables covered with a sauce.

"Show us how to handle this lobster shell Tom!" McAllister exclaimed.

Tom took a steak knife and cut away the shell for one of the ladies. He then took a fork and cut a piece of lobster tail, dipped it in the hot butter and handed it to the young lady.

"Oh my good Lord! This tastes so good!"

Tom cut away the remainder of the shells and removed them from the table. The guests went on and on about the lobster tails and steak filets. They even dipped the steak in the hot butter causing Tom to return to the table several times with refills.

George stood up with his glass of wine and offered a toast.

"Here's to Bill and the best damn meal I have ever had."

Before anyone could sit down, Sarah added, "And here is to the kitchen."

"Yes, and to the kitchen" Jed repeated.

When Sarah sat down, McAllister told Sarah in a whisper that it was very thoughtful of her to include the kitchen in the toast.

"Speaking of the kitchen, how many of you have had lemon pie?" Bill asked.

Everyone looked around and shrugged their shoulders.

"Lemon is so bitter" one of the ladies said.

"Not this lemon pie. It has a little something on top to take care of that. My cooks made me a lemon pie last week and it was so good, I ate the whole thing myself."

"Bring on the lemon pie!" one of the girls shouted.

Everyone was getting a little drunk as they laughed and demanded lemon pie. The pie came and they all dug in with their forks.

"Oh my! What is on top?!" one of them asked.

"It is some form of whipped cream" Bill replied.

"I do not wish to be rude Bill, but could you spare another slice?"

Bill and the girls laughed so hard that people on the saloon floor looked around. Bill asked if there was anyone else. Tom brought four more slices for the men and a slice for one of the girls.

"Jesus, Bill! How much do you want for those Chinese?" one of the men asked.

"They are very high priced and not for sale. If I sold them to you, I would have to travel all the way to Havre just for a slice of lemon pie!"

Sarah laughed along with everyone to make it look good. When they were done laughing, everyone took to the dance floor. There was so much smoke you could hardly see the piano player at the far end of the room. Sarah loved to dance and had a good time dancing with the other three guests. Bill was enjoying himself as he managed to dance with the other three girls before they all went back to the table for more drinks.

When eleven o'clock came, Bill and Sarah left for their private quarters. The six guests at the table said they would be leaving early in the morning and thanked Bill for the wonderful meal.

Once inside, Bill fell into a chair at the table and unbuttoned the top buttons of his shirt.

"I think I am ready for a nice glass of brandy" Bill said.

Sarah went to the liquor cabinet and came back to the table with a bottle of brandy, a bottle of liqueur and two glasses. She filled up the two glasses and made a toast.

"Here is to a wonderful evening!" Sarah exclaimed. They sipped on their drinks and took the stairs to make use of the two bedrooms.

In the morning, McAllister got dressed and nudged Sarah until she was awake.

"I am going over to the livery to get a report on the evening. I will join you later at the big table. Take your time, it is only seven o' clock."

"I will see you at the big table."

Sarah got out of bed, filled the tub and added the bubble soap.

"This is the last time I will have to scrub the slime off from that rotten son of a bitch" Sarah whispered.

After a good scrubbing, Sarah got into her riding clothes and went downstairs to the big table. She was amazed at how clean and tidy the saloon was. The Chinese were still in the kitchen cleaning and washing. Sarah could not talk to them because the two whites who worked the bar were busy writing in a book and counting money.

Sarah got a cup of coffee and went outside. A few people were out in front of the livery saying goodbye before they rode east. A deputy brought out three cowboys from the jail and ordered them to the west range. Bill waved at Sarah and walked across the street to greet her.

"That was a marvelous night Sarah" Bill said with a gleam in his eyes.

"Well, it was our last great evening for a while so I thought I would make it as enjoyable as possible Bill."

"I am going to miss you Mrs. McAllister."

Sarah took a gulp of coffee and could hardly get it down.

"Mrs. McAllister. I can hardly wait! Too bad I have to go to Winnipeg but the bank wants me to sign some papers before I get my money. The money I could leave but I have relatives I have to visit with before I leave. They will be coming to the wedding!"

"How nice! It will be good to meet them!" Bill exclaimed.

"Yes. I know you are going to enjoy them. They are very religious Bill, so I hope there will be no whores around."

"There will be no whores!"

"How long do you think you will be gone?" Bill asked.

"Maybe two weeks or a little more. Too bad we have to go back to Havre and wait for different trains."

"But you do not have to go back to Havre. If you ride almost straight north, ranchers will put you on a trail to a place called Cut Bank. According to some of the speculators, there is a town just north of the border called Lethbridge. From there, you can catch a train that takes you clear across Canada!" McAllister exclaimed.

"How wonderful! I will be back in less than two weeks for sure!"

"I will start getting ready for the wedding right away!"

"Now, wait until I get back before you start the guest list! I do not want any drunk cowboys or whores there!"

"I will wait!" Bill said with a laugh.

McAllister told Sarah to wait for him at the big table while he picked up the money from the saloon and the bank to put in the vault. Sarah told McAllister not to be long and stayed on the planks to finish her coffee.

I think I will tell Michael and mother about this wedding. I will pull them aside to make sure they are surprised and give us their blessings. This will cinch the deal" Sarah whispered to herself.

Sarah went into the saloon and waited for McAllister. When he arrived, she told him what she had decided.

"That might be a good idea" McAllister agreed.

"I am so excited Bill!"

"Well, it is now just a little after ten o'clock. They should be coming soon. What if your mother does not approve? There is an age difference you know."

"She will approve! She is the one who thought I should get a more mature man and the fact that you can support a wife does not hurt either. If she does not approve, then I guess she will not be coming to the wedding."

"Sarah, you are one in a million. I love you very much!"

"I meant to ask you, what do those three men at the big table do for a living?"

"They are land speculators. The one called Jed bought a fair chunk of land from me a while back."

McAllister stopped to laugh.

"The railroad went in the other direction and I bought the land back from him for less than half of the amount he paid me. It was a very nice stroke of business.

Anyhow, he got the proper information from the right people and asked me to form a fifty/fifty partnership with him."

"That was nice of him" Sarah said.

"Not really. He needed money."

"And how has it worked out?" Sarah asked.

"Beyond my wildest expectations!"

"Who are the other two?"

"They are planners. They lay out towns according to specifications. Towns are good! There are so many small parcels to sell."

"Do they come often?"

"Yes, just about every week. Jed cannot buy or sell anything without my signature."

"Are you not worried that he will get your signature and not come back?"

"No, I have the documents with both our signatures in the vault. When he brings half the money for the sale, I give him the documents. The money he brings is called a draft which he will deposit in my account in Havre. I get paid up front and he gets the back half."

"How do the other two get paid?"

"I pay them half of their fee from my share and Jed pays them the balance."

"So that is why you spend so much time with them in the bank!" Sarah shouted.

"Yes, and it is always a pleasure to entertain them. They leave a hundred dollars each for the good times."

"Oh my God! They paid for our dinners and wine!"

"Of course!"

After breakfast, McAllister spoke with the two bartenders before they left and gave them a sum of money. They waved to Sarah as they left and Sarah waved back.

McAllister returned and brought two fresh cups of coffee from the bar.

"I sure hope you are not just fooling about this wedding Bill. It would break my heart."

"Have no fear my love. Wait for me in the living quarters and I will be back in just a few minutes."

Sarah went to the living quarters and when McAllister returned, he was hiding something under his jacket. He took his hand from under his jacket and raised a half brick of gold in the air.

"This is one half brick of pure gold! After we are married, I will give you the other half brick to complete the wedding gift."

"Oh my God! I am going to put it under my pillow every night and think of you Bill!"

"Maybe you should leave it here where it is safe" McAllister suggested.

"I couldn't! It is kinda like an engagement ring!"

"Well I guess . . . . I guess . . . . Well, if you look at it like that, I think you should have it with you. Yes! I agree and happy engagement!"

"It is so precious! I am not going to show it to anyone until I get the other half!"

Sarah took the half brick upstairs and came down with it in her saddle bag. She threw her arms around Bill and thanked him several times. Bill scratched his head as Sarah went on about how generous he was.

"No use wasting a perfectly good day. Let us enjoy the sunshine out on the planks."

"Good idea. They will be here soon" Sarah said.

Chapter Eighteen

Anne Buys the West Ranch

"The nation will get the money back after the massacre."

In less than one half hour Michael and Anne appeared on the horizon. Sarah poked McAllister to get his attention. Sarah jumped up and down and waved both arms.

"I am going to walk out and tell them the good news!" Sarah exclaimed.

"I will wait here."

McAllister watched them approach and dismount. After they embraced, he saw Sarah pull her mother aside and engage in a conversation.

"Now listen, I know all about the McAllister operation." Sarah continued, "We have plenty of time to discuss it but right now, I will tell you I made a promise to marry McAllister."

Anne's mouth opened and was she was speechless.

"Do not worry. I had to keep him off the trail. I need you and Michael to give me hugs and kisses. He told me about a north route to Lethbridge and Calgary on our way to Winnipeg. I will mention it. Now give me more hugs!"

McAllister watched them embrace again but this time with more enthusiasm. He smiled for he knew Sarah told her mother and she approved.

When they reached the planks, Sarah rushed to embrace McAllister.

"Well Mr. McAllister, a great deal has happened since I left."

"Please, just call me Bill."

"Well Bill, I only have one daughter so I think we should talk before I purchase one of your ranches."

"You found a ranch?"

"Yes, the first one we saw."

"You mean the Wilson ranch?"

"Yes" Anne replied.

"Mother I am so happy for you!" Sarah exclaimed.

"Well Anne, we can all go to my living quarters and discuss the wedding and the ranch."

"Just the three of us will be fine. Michael will take the horses to the livery for feed and water."

"Sarah, maybe your mother would like to freshen up and have a drink. I will have Tom put some breakfast on the big table while I gather up the documents for the Wilson ranch."

"Sounds good Bill!" Sarah exclaimed.

Sarah and Anne went inside and Michael left for the livery. He told them he would be back soon for breakfast.

Anne went upstairs and splashed her face with water while Sarah waited for her.

When Anne returned, they left for the big table where Michael was eating breakfast. Tom's wife came to the table with two more plates of bacon and eggs along with cups of coffee.

"Thank you" Anne said.

Tom's wife smiled and left as McAllister joined the table. Anne and Sarah spoke of the wedding and guests as though McAllister was not even there. It pleased McAllister to know that Anne and Sarah were excited. Michael could care less and just kept eating.

"We could probably use a little more coffee" McAllister said.

"I will get it. Would you like bacon and eggs Bill?" Sarah asked.

"Thank you but I will have dinner a little later."

"I could do with just a little more bacon" Michael stated.

"Of course. Do you mind bringing your brother a little more bacon Sarah?"

"Coming right up!"

Sarah went to the kitchen where Tom was waiting.

"I heard your brother and the bacon is heating. I was there when McAllister got rid of his wife for a younger woman. He told her he worked too hard for everything he owned. He told her she could leave with her life, the clothes on her back and twenty dollars for a train ticket. I took her by buggy to Havre.

He is a snake. Be careful Miss Sarah."

"He will soon be a dead snake. Remember, ten days or so in the middle of the night."

"We are ready Sarah."

Sarah returned to the big table with the coffee and bacon. They were still talking about guests when Sarah arrived.

"Well, there is lots of time to plan for this wedding when we get back. Right now, I would like to know if we buy the Wilson ranch or keep on looking. We have a lot of riding to do before dark."

"I understand" McAllister said.

"Michael, would you mind getting the horses saddled?"

"Yes, just as soon as I am done with the bacon."

McAllister, Anne and Sarah proceeded to the living quarters.

"Well, let me see now. This is the third sale of the property and the title is still registered under the name of Wilson. I have signed the foreclosure papers that puts the property in my name so all I have to do is sign off my legal ownership to you for monies paid."

"And how much money will that be?"

"The last sale was to Wilson for three hundred dollars and he built a pretty fair ranch house and barn. How did you like the buildings?"

"They need some work but all in all, they are very good" Anne replied.

"I think a fair price would be five hundred dollars" McAllister stated.

"In all fairness Bill, you did not have to do much riding to make this sale. I am prepared to pay you four hundred dollars cash right now."

McAllister leaned back in his chair and smiled.

"Sarah said you have money and I am beginning to understand why" Bill stated.

"Well Bill, that is my offer. If you like, I can take a look at a few more ranches."

"I don't think that will be necessary. What the hell, we are going to be more than neighbors soon. You are going to need livestock. Correct?"

"Yes, probably about twenty cows, two strong bulls, two mares and a good stud" Anne replied.

"Well, here is the deal. If you promise to buy the livestock from me at the going rate, I will agree to four hundred dollars for the ranch" McAllister stated.

"It sounds good to me. It would be less expensive for me to buy the livestock from you at the going price than to chase all over Montana" Anne said.

"Then it's a deal! Would you like to close the deal with a drink?"

"I do not drink" Anne said.

"This is so wonderful! We will be able to ride in from the ranch and help with the wedding!" Sarah exclaimed.

McAllister showed Anne the documents and they both signed them.

"Did Sarah give you two hundred dollars for safe keeping?"

"Yes she did."

"I see Michael is outside with the horses. Would you go to the saddle bags and bring in two hundred dollars, Sarah?"

"I sure will!" Sarah exclaimed.

"This is my only daughter. I sure hope you treat her with respect Bill."

"You can count on it Anne!" Bill exclaimed.

Sarah returned with two hundred dollars and Bill gave Anne a receipt for payment in full. Sarah went upstairs for a few of her personal items and returned downstairs just as Anne was going out the door.

"Just a hug Bill, my mother is very strict. Oh yes, could you do something for me while I am gone?"

"Anything" Bill said with a big smile.

"I do not want your wife or daughter's jewelry or clothes. Could you have the Chinese box them before I get back?"

"It will be done right away. We can sell them in Havre when we go there for your diamonds" Bill added.

Bill stepped out on the planks and gave Sarah a hug before they rode away."

"See you in two weeks!" McAllister shouted.

"Less than that!" Sarah shouted back.

When they reached the slopes, Sarah looked back to see McAllister still on the planks and she gave a final wave.

"Jesus! I could not have stayed another day!"

"I know. Did you get the information Chief Dalton wanted?" Anne asked.

"Yes. I know his entire operation including where he keeps the money."

About one thirty, they met the riders Dalton sent to meet them. Michael told them Sarah wanted to see the ranch that the nation bought and would ride to the village in the morning.

They spoke for a while and the riders rode northwest to the village.

"Tell Chief Dalton we did not have to use the Flathead story" Michael said.

"After you see the Wilson ranch, there is a stream nearby where we can camp for the night" Anne said.

"I think you are going to like the ranch" Michael added.

"The ranch is in my name but it was paid for with nation money. It belongs to the nation" Anne stated.

"The nation will get the money back after the massacre" Sarah said.

"Yes I suppose so. Weddings are so enjoyable. Everyone is in such good spirits and there is music, dancing and lots to eat."

"Wedding? What are you talking about?! There is no wedding!" Sarah exclaimed.

"I'm sorry. Of course! I don't know why I mentioned a wedding Sarah."

Michael smiled and rode his horse ahead. After a few hours and with the ranch house in sight, Michael told them he would ride to the camp site and scare up some food.

When they arrived at the camp site, Michael had the fire going and was cleaning a fish down by the stream.

"My this is beautiful. Is this where you and Michael camped?"

"Yes. Twice."

"How did you like the ranch house?" Michael asked as he walked up the slope.

"The ranch house is beautiful! What a big fireplace!" Sarah exclaimed.

Michael and Anne looked at one another.

"Sarah, right behind those rocks over there is a nice sandy shore. We will put the horses out to graze and get supper started if you want to splash around for a while" Michael offered.

"Yes, that sounds good to me!"

Sarah went to her saddle bags and returned with her doe skins and gave Michael two bottles of wine.

"Good Lord! This will be great with supper" Michael shouted.

They all had a good laugh as Sarah headed for the stream.

"You have to tell Sarah about us" Michael said.

"I know. I will tell her after we are done eating."

After the horses were hobbled and Sarah returned from the stream, they all sat around a flat stone eating from the fry pan and passing a bottle of wine.

"Let's open that other bottle!" Sarah exclaimed.

"I am going to take a quick swim. Don't drink it all before I get back."

Michael went to the stream while the girls cleaned up the camp and opened the other bottle.

"Michael and I want to get married and settle down on the ranch we just saw" Anne said.

"What! When did this happen?"

"In the last few days."

"What about father?" Sarah asked.

"Well, you know what your father is up to as well as I do. You are the one who told me to leave. Remember?"

Yes, but I kinda thought you might go east with me or at least go to Calgary. I did not think you would leave father for another man."

"I do not want to go to Calgary or anywhere else. I want to stay close to the mountains and your grandparents. The ranch is just a few hours from the village and Michael and me might have enough money to buy it from the nation."

"Jesus! I have enough money to buy it from the nation!"

Anne shook her head and looked away but could not hold back her laughter.

"How many more daughters like you are out there?!" Anne said with a laugh.

Sarah took a swig from the bottle and handed it to her mother.

"Well, leaving is leaving! Leave alone or leave with a man, what difference does it make" Sarah stated.

"I am glad you know. Do you approve?"

"You should have left a long time ago" Sarah answered.

"Did you bang McAllister?"

"Bang! Where did you hear bang?" Sarah asked.

"Michael picked it up at the Fort."

"Jesus! Of course I banged the son of a bitch! Did you bang Michael?"

"Of course!"

There was silence and then laughter as the two embraced.

"I am going to take this bottle and sit over there under that tree. There is just enough left for me."

Michael returned from his swim and spoke with Anne. He was happy to hear that Sarah more or less approved of their wedding plans.

"We had better go visit with Sarah and see if we can get a drink. If she finishes that bottle by herself, she will not be able to ride tomorrow" Michael stated.

Sarah sat under her tree taking swigs. She pointed her finger at them and shouted, "Bang! Bang!"

Michael and Anne were still laughing as they sat down beside Sarah and with a little coaxing, Sarah passed the bottle around.

They left early in the morning so they could reach the village in time for dinner.

"We have seven Chinese to take with us" Sarah said.

"Seven Chinese!" Michael exclaimed.

"Yes, almost eight. Tom's wife is due in three months" Sarah said.

"Why do we have to get them out?" Michael asked.

"Because if we do not take them, we have to kill them." Sarah continued, "Chief Piapot and your father will not allow them to be killed. Besides, I told them we would take them with us to Canada."

"Since when did you get to decide?" Michael asked.

"Since I banged a greedy slimy pig!" Sarah shouted.

There was silence as they rode.

It was just before noon when they reached the village. Dalton, Beth and Wandering Buffalo were first to greet them. There were hugs all around and after a few words, they went to the forge for dinner.

"Oh my! This place looks huge when it is empty" Anne exclaimed.

"Yes. All of the Chiefs are suggesting it be made into a church from May until the end of October." Dalton continued, "David Stonebreaker is a man of the cross and is allowed to marry people. David wants to come and Chief Piapot likes the idea very much. It is something we will discuss after we return from the Yankee Territory."

"I am so excited!" Anne continued, "But how can he be a priest? He is married with children."

"He is not a priest. He just wears a black suit and has a shirt with a white collar" Dalton explained.

"Where is Big Man? I guess he didn't know we were coming?" Anne said.

Dalton paused. "He knew you were coming."

Dalton left with some food and went to the planks to speak with Sarah and Michael. They told Dalton about the ranch and the Chinese.

"The riders I sent told me about the ranch but they did not tell me about the Chinese. Sarah was right to tell them, Chief Piapot would not allow them to be killed and I feel the same way.

There is much to be discussed. The dog soldiers have given many suggestions and I will call a meeting for nine o'clock tomorrow morning. I want you and Sarah to be there. Right now the village is just going to celebrate your safe return, especially you Sarah."

"Where is my father?"

"He knew you would be here."

Dalton looked at his boots as Sarah left to find her mother.

As Sarah approached, she could see her mother and father speaking. She turned around and left for the forge where she met up with her grandparents. Beth told Sarah how worried they were. Sarah loved her grandparents and after a short visit, she gave them both a hug before she left to meet with what was left of the younger crowd.

"I saw Big Man here" Michael said.

"Yes, I saw them talking. I guess we will know soon about your plans" Sarah stated.

"Do you still approve of our plans?"

"Yes. But I just hope everyone can remain friends" Sarah replied.

"We will always be friends Sarah. I like you and your mother very much."

"I will go along with whatever is decided," Sarah continued. "I will go back now and find out what is happening. See you tomorrow morning."

Chapter Nineteen

Preparing for the Massacre

"The Chinese will be out before sunrise."

In the morning, the council along with Michael, Sarah and Anne met at the Wandering Buffalo Lodge.

"Chief Raincloud! How many dog warriors are ready to go south?" Dalton asked.

"At least seventy-five" Raincloud answered.

"Now we already have maps of the east and west ranges. I want the three who went south to bring a map of the settlement. You can leave now and return here tomorrow morning with the map. From now on, all meetings will begin at nine o'clock in the morning.

Along with the map, I want an estimate of how many gunfighters and deputies McAllister has working for him. I want to know their location and the location of the Chinese" Dalton ordered.

Anne, Sarah and Michael got up and left.

"Benjamin! How many have you trained with the dynamite?" Dalton asked.

"Six and I make seven."

"That should be enough. We have to deal with a dam, maybe a vault and a building or two" Dalton stated.

"Seven is enough. The dam will only take three" Benjamin said.

"Chief Big Man Walking! We will use the ranch house for the wounded. How many will you need to assist you?"

"Maybe five or six."

"You can tell us tomorrow morning if you have found the assistants you need."

Big Man nodded.

"Chief Raincloud! How many warriors will you need to take over the town?"

"We need two to the east and two on the west road to make sure no one gets out and no one gets in. I will be with the four in town and we need four more for the east ranch house."

Dalton nodded his head and smiled.

"I guess you all know that we have seven and one half Chinese to clear out of there" Dalton stated.

"One half?"

"Yes. One of the girls is having a baby!"

There was a roar of laughter.

"Chief Wandering Buffalo! How many will you need for these people and three wagons?" Dalton asked.

"Four should be enough. We will take them out before the sun comes up."

"Good! Now the gunfighters out on the west range are something we will wait to talk about until we meet with the map makers tomorrow morning. Thunderchild and the dog warriors will take care of the gunfighters on the west range.

We have over one thousand five hundred head of cattle and horses to move.

Now I know you have been wondering why Gordon Strong is here. He is here to tell us how to move this herd across the creek and into the Flathead nation. Go ahead, Gordon" Dalton said.

"You must divide the livestock into herds of about one hundred to get them started. Michael said the creek is just belly deep so this will not create a problem.

Now, cattle will balk and bunch up when they hit a creek. You have to round up a small herd of horses and drive them in front of the first small herd. The horses will run the creek and the cattle will follow. Once the first herd of cattle are in the water, there will be no problem with the rest.

If you have the riders, use five for each herd. That would be about seventy-five riders. Do you have seventy-five riders?"

"No problem! The Flatheads can give us forty riders" Dalton answered.

"Now it is like the old buffalo days. Move the front herds with speed. Take your time with the cattle in the rear so they do not bunch up and spread out.

The big hills on this map run east and west for a short distance. Cattle will not run the hills. Drive them west and east around the hills.

Are there any questions?"

"Not right now, maybe tomorrow though" Dalton stated.

There was laughter and everyone thanked Gordon for his help. The group visited for a while before going to the Forge.

On the way, Dalton stopped to talk with Benjamin Stonebreaker.

"Our two young scouts are in the Flathead nation. The Flatheads are going to show them where we can hide over one and a half thousand head of livestock. According to the Flatheads, we can drive them through a narrow pass into a very large meadow.

The scouts will be here before supper. I think we should dynamite the pass once the cattle go through. Talk to the scouts when they arrive" Dalton suggested.

"I think we should definitely dynamite the pass and it is something we can set up for right now before we go south" Benjamin said.

Dalton gave Benjamin a shoulder hit and left to find Thunderchild.

When Dalton found Thunderchild, they discussed the west range.

"I will get the dog warriors together and we will decide how we are going to divide the herd and get to the south side. I will be anxious to take a look at the maps in the morning. We have to know where the gunfighters' bunkhouses are" Thunderchild stated.

Dalton nodded and they walked to the Forge.

Nine o'clock the next morning, Raincloud told Dalton that the Benjamin party left at sun up with the two scouts to prepare the dynamite for the pass.

Dalton nodded and sat down at the long table. Michael gave Dalton a map which located the west range ranches and bunkhouses.

"How many gunfighters are on the west range?" Thunderchild asked.

"Forty to forty-five" Michael replied.

"How do you know?"

"Sarah counted them" Michael replied.

Thunderchild smiled, took the map and rose from the table to meet with the dog warriors.

"Thunderchild! You do not have to come in the mornings until you are close to a plan."

Thunderchild nodded and left.

"Big Man! Tomorrow morning you will take your assistants and supplies to the ranch. When you go through the Flathead nation, several Flathead warriors and their women will join you. The ranch house needs cleaning."

Big Man Walking left the meeting.

"Sarah! Tell us about the settlement and the deputies" Dalton said.

"During the week, there are four deputies in the settlement, two sleep above the store and two are across the street in the deputies' office and small jail. Four are out at the east ranch beside the road. All eight of them are in town on Friday and Saturday."

"We will be going to the settlement on Wednesday of next week. Continue" Dalton stated.

"Now the paper money, gold bricks and thin plates, silver dollars and titles to all the land are not in the bank" Sarah stated.

"Where then?" Wandering Buffalo asked.

"Everything is in a vault. Only about five hundred dollars is left in the bank."

"Did you say gold bricks?" Dalton asked.

"Yes. Lots of them" Sarah replied.

"Where is the vault?" Wandering Buffalo asked.

"Do you see the hallway leading from the bank to the living quarters?" Sarah asked.

"Yes" they replied.

"The vault is in the hallway four of my big steps from the door leading to the bank. There is a picture on the wall. If you remove the picture, there is a square hole with a latch on the inside. You can just put your hand in and lift the latch. The paneling turns into a door and when the door opens you will find the steel door to the vault. It has a combination lock that only McAllister can open."

"Good! We will take McAllister alive and I will make him open the door!" Raincloud exclaimed.

"That will not work!"

"Why not?" Dalton asked.

"Because the door is on a timer set for twelve o'clock. Not even McAllister can get the door open before then" Sarah explained.

"Jesus!" Dalton shouted.

Sarah continued, "The vault is made of concrete and steel on all four sides. The inside is lined with steel plates and the ceiling too. To get through the door, you would have to use so much dynamite there would be nothing left inside the vault except maybe the gold bricks."

"Well, how the hell are we going to handle this?!" Raincloud shouted.

"There is another way. The steel panels on the ceiling are supported on the inside with pieces of steel placed on an angle. The steel plates are just lying across the narrow side of the vault resting on the concrete walls. I went upstairs and took four steps from the west bedroom wall. The bed is against the north wall right over the vault. All you have to do is haul the bed to one side, remove the planks and a couple of the steel panels and you are inside the vault."

There was silence and then a roar of laughter.

"This is my granddaughter!" Wandering Buffalo shouted.

They all took turns giving Sarah hugs. Michael and Anne laughed as her feet dangled with each hug.

Dalton told two of the assistants to bring a keg of wine and mugs. They were still laughing and praising Sarah when the two assistants returned with the keg.

They were having such a good time, none of them even left to go for dinner.

After a few drinks, everyone started getting hungry and left for the Forge.

"I cannot get over how different this place looks. It is hard to believe that just a few days ago, we had a Great Hall and swimming pools." Sarah continued, "Even the lodges are gone. My grandfather's lodge is the only one left."

"Yes, and that will be gone soon" Dalton added.

"The Forge has hot water. I thought they were going to stop the hot water from coming down" Michael stated.

"And there are latrines left and right of the fire bed and Stone wall" Anne said.

"Well, I guess the Forge is going to be a church and hot water coming down continually will clean the latrines."

"My mother thinks the church is going to be the best thing we have done!" Anne exclaimed.

The four arrived at the planks and went in different directions.

Michael had a chance to talk alone with Anne and asked her about Big Man.

"He definitely wants to live in Calgary. I think that is where he will go after the massacre. I told him I would not be going with him and he did not seem too upset."

"I miss you, Michael!"

"I miss you too." Michael continued, "When this McAllister thing is over, we are going to the little white church and then to the ranch."

They both smiled and went for something to eat.

The next morning was Wednesday, just one week away from the attack on McAllister and his hired guns. Dalton agreed to be in charge of the attack on the east ranch and join Raincloud in the town when they were done.

Anne and Sarah insisted they be part of the attack on the town and Dalton told them he would have an answer on Thursday.

In the afternoon, Thunderchild spoke with the council about the west range.

"The Stonebreaker party will return today or tomorrow for sure. The women are putting together food now and there will be no reason to hunt.

Sunday morning, we will go to the Flathead nation and stay there until Tuesday. We will take Michael, the Stonebreaker party and the two young scouts with us" Thunderchild stated.

"Yes, we are leaving Sunday as well" Dalton added.

"The two young scouts speak the Flathead tongue. According to Anne and Michael, there is one large hill on the west range. They did not go there but said that from the top of the hill, we would be able to see everything including the bunkhouses.

On Monday I will take the scouts and Michael to the top of the hill. Before morning on Wednesday, I will take the dog warriors through the herd and reach the south shore ending up between the two bunkhouses. Half of us will attack the bunkhouse to the west and the other half will attack the bunkhouse to the east.

Now, the Flatheads and our warriors, who will herd the cattle, will follow behind us and take one half of the herd east and the other half west. There will be no noise until they hear us dynamite the bunkhouses. We will need two from the Stonebreaker party.

I will put two warriors to the west and two warriors to the east just in case a few try to make a run for it. Now for the same reason, I will leave ten warriors spread out below the hills.

If there are gunfighters camping on the range, they will be caught in the stampede for the cattle will be moving fast once the dynamite explodes.

There will be no problem getting the cattle around the hills to the west. As the cattle stampede, they will come to a marsh caused by the dam. When they reach the marsh, they will follow the range around the hills and turn east. They will be tired by then and with nothing chasing them, they will slow down before crossing the creek with the herd from the east.

Do not forget, the Flatheads will be armed and they will know enough to join the massacre if it is necessary."

"It will not be necessary! You have a good plan, Thunderchild!" Dalton continued, "Send about twenty warriors to the settlement when you have everything under control. Michael said there are more than ten wagons outside the corral. We will need the wagons to haul away anything of value.

When we are just about finished, I will send a rider to tell Benjamin to dynamite the dam."

Thunderchild nodded and left for the gun range.

On Thursday, the council met with Sarah and Anne. "It has been decided that you will both ride to the McAllister settlement. When Chief Raincloud is in position, you will remain hidden in the brush overlooking the settlement until the fighting is over. Chief Raincloud will wave his rifle when it is time for you to ride down" Dalton stated.

Sarah and Anne nodded their approval.

"Tell me Sarah, what is there of value besides what is in the vault."

"In all the rooms, including McAllister's living quarters, there are all kinds of nice blankets and of course beds if you are interested."

"Maybe. What else?" Wandering Buffalo asked.

"There is very much wine, beer and whiskey in the saloon and the private living quarters. Also, the kitchen has very many pots, pans and dishes."

"I do not know about the dishes but the rest we will take. There will be twenty warriors coming from the west range to help us" Dalton stated.

"What is in the store?" Raincloud asked.

"Very many rifles, hand guns, ammunition, tobacco and small items. The livery is full of everything you will need for the wagons. There are teams of horses in the corral" Sarah added.

"The horses we will let out before the shooting starts. The twenty riders who come from the west range will be riding horses trained to the wagon" Dalton said.

"Thank you, my girl" Wandering Buffalo said.

"Grandfather, I told McAllister to box up the jewelry in the ranch house and there is also whiskey in his private bar. Tom will go with you to the ranch house."

Everyone told Sarah what a big help she was. Sarah gave her grandfather a hug and left with her mother.

"We cannot take those wagons through the mountains and foothills and we cannot take them on the plains" Dalton said.

"We will go for something to eat and talk about it after dinner" Wandering Buffalo said.

Everyone agreed and left the Lodge.

When they reached the Forge, Benjamin and the two scouts were back in camp.

"What did the pass look like?" Raincloud asked.

"Perfect! The pass is wide enough for the livestock and the walls have Stones, trees and mud. The great thing about the pass is that the walls are high and straight.

It is not necessary to bring down both sides. It will look more natural if only one side comes down" Benjamin stated.

"How are you going to light the dynamite" Dalton asked.

"We went half way up one side and dug three large holes. When the livestock pass, we will climb the other side of the pass and shoot the dynamite into the holes."

"Jesus! That is perfect!" Dalton exclaimed.

"We took a look at the meadow just like you asked us, Chief Dalton" one of the scouts said.

"How did it look?" Dalton asked.

"It couldn't be better. The meadow is sheltered and goes for miles. A creek runs through and empties into a lake miles away. To the north of the meadow, the hills are low and lead to the plains not far from the village. The Flatheads say we can take our half of the livestock whenever we want."

"Good. We will take them out about one hundred at a time and drive them to Gordon's Ranch. Gordon will market the livestock" Dalton explained.

"Now what about the wagons" Raincloud continued. "Is the pass wide enough for the wagons?"

"Oh yes."

"Good! Then that is how we will get the wagons to the village. We will give the Flatheads a little cash and some of the goods but no whiskey" Dalton stated.

"The Chinese will be out before sunrise. Should we take them through the pass?" Wandering Buffalo asked.

"No. Take them by horseback from the ranch house to our village. Leave the wagons and bring the goods by pack horse" Dalton said.

"I guess we do not need a meeting" Raincloud said.

Dalton and Raincloud sat down on the edge of the planks and ate soft biscuits with their mugs of raspberry wine. Dalton turned around and asked one of the young assistants to bring Gordon.

Gordon soon appeared and they spoke about how they would market the livestock.

"According to Michael's report, there will be only a few cattle with brands. These we will divide with the Flatheads and put to our own use." Dalton continued, "I think there will be over one thousand head of livestock to be sold. I say over one thousand because the Flatheads will not be able to sell their share of the livestock so we will have to sell them as well. We will buy their share from them at a fair price."

"Are you able to market this much livestock?" Dalton asked.

"Yes. I have a reputation as a cattle buyer. If you bring them in small herds, I will sell them in Lethbridge and Calgary. Do not forget, Heather's sister and brother-in-law are located near Calgary. Buying and selling cattle is what they do" Gordon added.

"It would cost money to ship them so less cattle to them and more to you" Raincloud stated.

This brought much laughter.

"How much would you need for your services?" Dalton asked.

"I think ten percent plus out of pocket expenses for shipping to Calgary and things like that."

"Ten percent plus disbursements sounds good to me. What about you, Chief Raincloud?"

Raincloud nodded.

"Disbursements?" Gordon asked.

"Yes. I picked that word up from Landsdown."

"I should have known!" Gordon exclaimed.

There was more laughter as they left for steaks and raspberry wine.

In the afternoon, Wandering Buffalo and Beth along with Anne and Sarah, spoke with Dalton.

"Instead of tearing down our lodge, we would like to make it a summer home for David and Mary. Benjamin said he could bring in hot and cold water. Also, there are enough Stones to build a latrine and a fireplace" Beth said.

"Tell Benjamin he must hide the hot water line as he did in the Forge" Dalton stated.

"Then it is a deal?!" Beth shouted.

"Well, what can I do! You have the whole family against me!"

The whole family praised Dalton and there were hugs all around.

Gordon joined them and as they walked down to the garden, Dalton asked about the builders at the Trading Post.

"They are finished with the Trading Post" Gordon stated.

"Then where are they?" Dalton asked.

"I guess they stayed to do some work for some old guy who owns the livery" Gordon replied.

"Old Sam! Yes of course. We promised to fix him up with a fireplace or two and put in latrines. What about Vincent?"

"You mean the great Mr. Lugar?" Gordon asked.

Dalton smiled and nodded.

"He is doing just fine. According to Helen, the great Mr. Lugar is walking around town with bankers and builders paying more for steaks and wine than it is worth. Everyone calls him Mr. Lugar!" Gordon exclaimed.

Dalton could not help but laugh as they made their way down the hidden trail to the garden.

"There is something good about this massacre" Sarah said.

"What is it?" her grandfather asked.

"Every last one of these people except McAllister, are wanted for either murder, bank robbery, horse stealing, cattle rustling and God only knows what else. Nobody is going to be looking for them except the law" Sarah stated.

"And if you talk to the people in Cut Bank, nobody will be looking for McAllister either" Dalton added.

"It is a good deal any way you look at it!" Gordon exclaimed.

Chapter Twenty

The Chinese Exodus

"Holy! They look like Mongolians!"

On Friday and Saturday, everyone in the village was busy preparing for the Sunday morning ride into Yankee Territory. Dried meat, jars of fruit and bags of potatoes were brought to the Forge. It would not be necessary to hunt until the massacre was over.

Dalton spoke to those in charge to make sure all the horses were shod and everyone wore boots. He asked each one if there were any questions. No one had any questions so Dalton went to the upper levels to soak in the hot pool and visit with Louise.

Early Sunday morning, Thunderchild took his warriors to the Forge and picked up the pack horses that were loaded with supplies. He made sure one of the horses had ammunition for the Flatheads.

Thunderchild sent his warriors south and stopped to talk with Dalton. He told Dalton they would set up camp at the Flathead nation and ride to the ranch Monday morning with the forty Flatheads who would help with the cattle. Thunderchild turned his horse and rode south.

Dalton and Raincloud went to where Benjamin Stonebreaker and his assistants were loading the dynamite. Benjamin left two of his assistants with Raincloud and Dalton before leaving.

The Dalton and Raincloud party rode east. Dalton wanted the young scouts to show him the pass. They rode east only a short distance before the scouts turned south.

"This is where we turn south to reach the meadows. I think the pass and meadows are north of the Yankee Territory. It will be about two hours before we reach the pass" the scout said.

As they rode south, the scouts came to a ridge and waved Dalton forward. Dalton and Raincloud rode to the ridge and stopped their horses alongside the scouts.

"There is the meadow and the pass is over there to the southeast corner. The creek runs west and turns south around those hills into the Flathead territory" the scout explained.

Raincloud and Dalton removed their glasses from the saddle bags. The remainder of the party reached the ridge and spoke to one another of how beautiful the meadow looked.

"This is just about as good as you can get it!" Raincloud said.

"Let us go look at the pass" Dalton said.

After a short ride, they reached the pass and rode through. As they rode, the two explosive assistants pointed out the three holes into which the bows would shoot the dynamite.

"This side of the pass is definitely coming down!" Dalton exclaimed.

"We are north of the Yankee border" Raincloud said.

"How do you know?" Dalton asked.

"I know the river that turns south. You must follow it south for a half day before you reach the Flathead nation" Raincloud replied.

Dalton nodded and the party rode southeast. By Monday afternoon, they set up camp less than two hours away from the McAllister settlement.

Everyone laughed as they unloaded the pack horses. They set up camp and hobbled the horses so they could graze before tying them for the night.

"We have enough steaks for everyone" Anne said.

"What about Piapot beets?" one of the dog warriors asked.

"Yes, we have Piapot beets!" Sarah replied.

The two young scouts took pleasure in helping Sarah get the food ready. Dalton and Raincloud set up a keg of wine and the raiding party ate four at a time.

After supper, the girls went to the stream and the four young riders brought in the horses. Anne and Sarah returned from the stream and helped finish the keg.

"When the keg is gone, there will be no more wine until we are done with McAllister and his gunfighters" Dalton stated.

Sarah and Anne almost spoke at the same time. They did not want McAllister killed.

"Do not kill McAllister until we come down to the settlement! I want to see his face when he finds out the truth!" Sarah exclaimed.

"We might have to kill him." Raincloud continued, "Does he have weapons in his living quarters?"

"He has two rifles on the wall downstairs and hangs his belt on a chair." Sarah continued, "If he goes to the ranch house, he will have only the weapons he takes."

"Does he go to the ranch house very often?" Dalton asked.

"No. I was there only once. He likes to be where his deputies are so he can be close to his money and give orders."

"What about the Chinese?" Raincloud asked.

"During the week, Tom and his wife go to the ranch at night and return early in the morning" Sarah replied.

"Tomorrow, we will watch the settlement until dark. I am sure we will know where he is" Raincloud stated.

"Yes, and tomorrow I will take my riders to the east ranch where some of the deputies sleep. When we are done with the deputies, we will burn the ranch house and ride west to the settlement.

Now remember, Anne, you and Sarah stay in the hills until we are finished with the settlement. Where do you think the deputies will be, Sarah?" Dalton asked.

"One or two will be in the deputy office and one or two will be sleeping above the store. The rest will be at the east ranch."

"What about the dynamite? We cannot use dynamite until we remove the money, rifles and whatever we are going to take" Raincloud stated.

"No. We can use half loads and use the dynamite in two places. We can dynamite the deputies' office and the rooms above the store. It should kill everyone who is close and whoever is still alive will be scrambling to get the hell out. They will not even look for their weapons."

"Good! I will take a warrior and we will find McAllister" Raincloud exclaimed.

"Everything will happen at six o'clock" Dalton stated.

They all sat around the fire discussing the attack until late in the evening. When the keg was empty, they gathered up their robes and went to sleep.

At the nation's ranch house, Thunderchild gave his final orders.

"Chief Wandering Buffalo, you and your riders will leave here at one o'clock. It is only a one hour ride to the Chinese bunkhouse. Make sure you leave there before three o'clock for we will begin moving the herd east and west at four o'clock."

Wandering Buffalo nodded and took his riders to a small campfire where they would sleep for a few hours.

Thunderchild spoke to the dog warriors and the Flatheads who would drive the herd.

"We know where the center of the herd is located. You people will follow my riders and move the herd east and west as we ride south.

We will be over the hills and in position at four o'clock and at six o'clock we will attack the bunkhouses. After six o'clock, you can make as much noise as you want. Kill anyone who survives the stampede."

At one o'clock, Wandering Buffalo saddled up and took his riders south.

"Why are you dressed like a cowboy, Chief Wandering Buffalo?" one of them asked.

"I do not want to scare the Chinese."

"You are sure scaring the hell out of us!"

They were still laughing as they crossed the creek.

When they arrived at the Chinese bunkhouse, Wandering Buffalo dismounted and knocked on the door. A young man opened the door and looked Wandering Buffalo up and down.

"Are you Tom?"

"Yes."

"Sarah sent us to take you out of here."

When they heard the name Sarah, there was laughter and tears. There was a commotion as they celebrated in Chinese and English.

"I am Sarah's grandfather. My name is Wandering Buffalo."

There was more commotion and celebrating.

"We must move now before the cattle run over us" Wandering Buffalo said.

"Is Sarah fine?" they asked.

"Yes. What about the teams?"

"We have been ready for the last two or three days. We have packed everything we are taking with us. The six horses are standing in the barn" Tom replied.

Wandering Buffalo ordered his riders to hook up the teams.

"Where is McAllister?"

"He is at the settlement. We must stop at the ranch house for some boxes" Tom stated.

"Yes, Sarah mentioned it."

Tom spoke to the brother-in-law and told him to take his younger brother to help with the teams. They left immediately.

"Your mother and father will ride with the girls in the covered wagon. Each of you men will take a wagon."

"Oh yes! That will be good!" Tom exclaimed.

"Do we have to break the door down or do you have a key?"

"Oh yes, Mr. Wandering Buffalo!"

Wandering Buffalo smiled as Tom reached in his pocket and handed him the key to the ranch house.

"I am beginning to understand why Sarah wanted to save you people."

"She is what the white man calls hero!" Tom exclaimed.

"I guess" Wandering Buffalo added.

The wagons soon arrived and one stopped in front of the ranch house. Wandering Buffalo rode over and opened the door. Several boxes were loaded and the three wagons headed south.

As they neared the creek, the wagons passed by the hundred warriors heading south. Wandering Buffalo stopped in the water and spoke with Thunderchild.

The warriors had long hair, painted faces and small braids on each side. They were heavily armed with Colts, Winchesters, and knives were strapped to their legs. Belts of ammunition hung around their shoulders.

The moonlight hit the water and the Chinese could see them pass.

"Holy! They look like Mongolians" one of them said nervously.

When the wagons reached the ranch house, everyone was waiting for them. Candles, lanterns and a burning fireplace lit the room. The Chinese were seated at a long table as plates of food arrived from the kitchen.

"There is coffee, tea and wine" Big Man said.

They spoke to each other in Chinese. "I would be happy with coffee. They would like tea" Tom explained.

When they were finished eating, Tom's father spoke to him in Chinese. Tom got to his feet and told everyone what his father said.

"Since my family came to this country, we have worked for the railroad and then McAllister. Each day my family has made food for the white man. This is the first time someone has made food and waited on us. So I will say Thank you for all you have done."

As Tom sat down, Wandering Buffalo walked by and gave the father a pat on the shoulder. A French wife started to cry and left for the kitchen.

"There is a large tent for the women and we have four buffalo robes for the men. You can sleep in the barn or outside by the fire" a young warrior stated.

After a short conversation, Tom said they would like to sleep outside by the fire.

Chapter Twenty-One

The McAllister Massacre

"You! . . . You! . . . You Bitch! You filthy slut! You Whore!"

Just before six o'clock, the cattle were divided and moving east and west. Michael looked at his watch and told his riders and the Flatheads to get ready.

With the west and east bunkhouses surrounded, Thunderchild looked at his watch and ordered the dynamite into the west bunkhouse. He watched from a distance as the dynamite smashed through a window. In just seconds, the bunk house exploded and the air was filled with debris and pieces of gunfighters.

Almost simultaneously, an explosion could be heard from the east bunk house.

Thunderchild watched as two gunfighters came out of the front door. One was crawling and the other one walked on one good leg. Winchesters fired and they were shot to pieces on the veranda planks.

Thunderchild ordered a second round of dynamite. The dynamite went into the center of the bunkhouse and blew out three walls and what was left of the roof. Shooting was heard around the bunkhouse as the warriors put bullets in the heads of what was left of the gunfighters and threw them into the burning bunkhouse.

Several warriors were hit by debris and one warrior on the south side was killed when his horse slipped in the mud and rolled on him. The wounded warriors were taken north to the ranch.

A few minutes later, two riders came from the east bunkhouse and reported to Thunderchild.

"The east bunkhouse is on fire and our warriors have killed all the gunfighters who made it out alive" one of them reported.

"Any of our warriors get killed?"

"Yes. Two gunfighters were in the small brush just east of the bunkhouse when we arrived. They got off a few shots before we killed them. Two of our riders are dead and one is wounded. They are taking him and the other two who were killed to the ranch.

"Any more wounded?" Thunderchild asked.

"Not while I was there."

"Ride back and take the warriors to the settlement to help out" Thunderchild ordered.

The two turned and left immediately. Thunderchild made sure everything was finished at the bunkhouse and took his warriors west to help out with the big herd.

When the warriors arrived at the settlement, the livery was on fire, and two wagons were out front being loaded with guns, ammunition, saddles, saddle blankets, bridles, harnesses and other items. The warriors left to help load the wagons in front of the saloon.

Out in front of the bank, Raincloud waved his rifle as an 'all clear' signal for Anne and Sarah. Dalton soon arrived without his riders.

"Jesus! Where are the rest?!" Raincloud asked.

"Everything is fine! The east ranch is burning and four dead deputies are going up in smoke. The other riders are bringing in about one hundred head of cattle from the east range. The cattle will follow behind to hide any wagon tracks to the pass."

"What about McAllister?" Dalton asked.

"McAllister is right where we want him, alive and tied to a pole. He was asleep when we went upstairs but he woke up and tried to get out a window. I shot him in the leg."

Sarah and Anne soon joined Raincloud and Dalton on the planks and the four went upstairs.

When they reached the bedroom, McAllister was foaming at the mouth and making threats.

"My deputies and gunfighters will be here soon and if you do not clear out, they will kill every one of you!" McAllister shouted.

"Your deputies and gunfighters are all dead" Dalton said.

McAllister looked around to where Dalton was standing with Sarah and Anne. His mouth dropped and his eyes opened wide with disbelief.

"I told you my relatives were coming to the wedding, Bill" Sarah said.

"You! . . .You! . . .You bitch! You filthy slut! You whore!" McAllister shouted.

Spit was coming out of his mouth and tears rolled down his face as McAllister continued his insults. Dalton and Raincloud walked to the vault area where the warriors were handing up gold bricks for they could not hold back their laughter.

When the last brick was handed up and put in a wooden box, Dalton asked if the vault was empty.

"Yes, the documents are in those boxes along with the paper money and coins" one of the warriors said.

The warriors began carrying out the boxes. Dalton and Raincloud walked over and talked to Sarah and Anne. McAllister slid down the pole and was now on his knees. He was still spitting out curses and threats but running out of steam.

Suddenly McAllister became silent as he slowly raised his face and looked Dalton square in the eyes.

"You are the one I made the deal with for the wagon loads of lumber" McAllister said.

"Yes." Dalton continued, "Sarah and Anne are the mother and sister to one of the boys you had killed in the ambush."

"You were supposed to come back with the wagons."

"I had other things to do" Dalton said.

"And you! You ride a solid black."

"Yes I do" Raincloud stated.

"The four boys killed one of your gunfighters and Chief Raincloud killed the other four" Dalton added.

"Yes. The informer told us to kill him first. The informer said his name was Death."

"So that is why the last gunfighter I killed called me Deathcloud" Raincloud said as he laughed.

"Now listen, if you set me free, I will give you some very valuable information. I am bleeding to death and even if I live, I will lose my leg."

Dalton could now see the lawyer side of McAllister starting to show.

"Both sides of his mouth" Dalton said to himself.

"I cannot even go to the law for I was implicated in having the four boys killed. They will hang me!"

"Hang you? For what? For killing four Indians? I do not think so, Bill."

"Yes, they will! I did not even want to ambush the boys! Hawk talked me into it!"

"Hawk?"

"Yes! Now you see, you do not even know his name. I can tell you what he looked like, what his horse looked like and where he went. Hawk wants you killed, Mr. Dillon, and he will not stop until you are dead. Do we have a deal?"

"I am very interested. Tell me about his horse" Dalton said.

The girls looked at Raincloud and Raincloud just smiled.

"Now let's be fair! I am being fair with you. I will write down everything about Hawk and leave it under a Stone just by the east road if you give me a start."

"All right. Here is the deal. You tell me what his horse looked like and we will take you with us. If you are right and we find Hawk, we will let you go."

There was a silence and then McAllister spoke.

"The horse was dark brown and well trained."

"Any markings?" Dalton asked.

"Yes. The horse had a white star and white socks on all four legs" McAllister said.

Dalton looked at the girls and motioned them to follow him. Raincloud and the girls followed Dalton to where the dynamite was being placed inside the vault.

"Well, if we were not sure before, we are now. It was Joseph" Raincloud said.

"Now I can give McAllister to the Flatheads so you girls could watch him suffer, if that is what you would like. I have seen enough of that kind of thing so I will not be there" Dalton stated.

"Neither will I" Raincloud added.

Sarah and Anne looked at McAllister kneeling on the floor blubbering like a child.

"What do you think we should do?" Anne asked.

"Put him in the vault and blow him all over the Montana territory" Dalton replied.

Anne nodded and left the room. Sarah looked at McAllister, nodded her head and followed her mother downstairs.

A warrior came to report that the wagons were loaded and heading north.

"What about the cattle?" Dalton asked.

"The cattle are here and following the wagons."

The two riders crawled out of the vault and stretched a long fuse from the vault to the top of the stairs. Raincloud ordered everyone to start burning the buildings and have the horses waiting.

"If he lied to me about the horse, I was going to give him to the Flatheads."

"I know" Raincloud said.

Dalton went behind the post and cut McAllister loose.

"We have to tie your legs and hands so you do not escape" Dalton explained.

"Oh thank God!" McAllister said.

When he was tied, they put a noose around his legs and dragged him over to the vault.

"What are you doing?!"

"We are doing you the biggest favour that anybody has ever done for you" Raincloud answered.

They tied the rope to a floor joist and lowered McAllister halfway down the vault. McAllister dangled in mid-air crying and begging.

Raincloud poured oil from the lamps on the north side of the floor while Dalton did the same at the bottom of the stairs. Raincloud lit the bottom of the stairs on fire and they both ran out the door.

They mounted up and everyone rode north with great speed. When they reached the top of the slope, they stopped and waited for the explosion. Dalton looked at his watch and it was fifteen minutes past seven.

They did not have to wait long. In just a few seconds, a mighty blast blew everything away in the center of the street.

When everything was almost burned to the ground, the two riders with the dynamite spoke to Dalton.

"We have enough dynamite to blow away the bank where the creek turns south to the bridge. We will also dynamite the bank south of the settlement" the young assistant continued.

"When the dam is blown, the water will flow straight through and it will be like the settlement never existed.

You can ride north and we will catch up with everyone when we are done."

Dalton nodded and rode northwest with the wagons and the cattle. As they moved along, Raincloud pointed to a high hill where they could view the west range. They rode up the hill and took a look at the west range with their glasses.

"My God! When Michael reported fifteen hundred head of livestock, he was right!" Raincloud exclaimed.

"The small herd has crossed the creek and the big herd from the west is closing fast" Dalton said.

"Yes, we had better get those wagons moving if we want to beat them to the pass" Raincloud added.

In less than an hour, they reached the pass. The wagons went through first followed by the cattle and horses. Raincloud took the wagon train north to the village and Dalton waited for the cattle from the west range.

While he was waiting, he heard several blasts of dynamite coming from the dam and the settlement. When he heard the blasts, he knew the cattle all crossed the creek and were close to the pass.

In a few minutes, about twenty horses came up the ravine pounding the shallow water in all directions.

"When the cattle come, we will send the horses through the pass. Gordon was right. They will follow the horses" Thunderchild said.

Did they balk at the creek?"

"Yes. But when we ran the horses in front, they followed right behind."

Thunderchild sent ten riders a short ways downstream to wait for the cattle. Dalton and the remaining riders spread out across the ravine so the horses and cattle would turn west into the pass.

In just minutes, the cattle started coming up the ravine. The ten riders waited until they were close and drove the twenty horses through the pass. The cattle turned and followed the horses.

It seemed like an endless flow of cattle. Dalton could see the last of the herd coming up the ravine and he looked at his watch. It was just past twelve o'clock.

When the last of the herd went through, the young assistants returned in time to shoot the dynamite into the holes on the south side of the pass. Three loud explosions could be heard causing a landslide of dirt, rocks and trees. Everyone had great praise for the young dynamite assistants as they joined the raiding party.

Dalton found the Flathead Chief and they discussed the dividing of the herd.

"We could take some of the cattle with brands. When winter comes, we will quarter them and pack horse the quarters to the butcher in Cut Bank. We have done business with him before and he is fair" the Flathead Chief stated.

"This is a large herd but we have more than ninety riders here. We will split the herd one hundred at a time. You take a hundred west and we will take one hundred north until the herd is divided equally."

"Did you lose any riders?" Dalton asked.

"Two were run into the bush and trampled to death when the cattle stampeded north after the dynamite went off. Some are wounded and went to the ranch."

"Yes. We also have two or three deaths. We stole money from the settlement and I will send you some" Dalton said.

"You do not have to because I know it was not part of the deal. Friendship is better than money."

The Flathead Chief smiled and rode west. Dalton met with Thunderchild and they discussed the herd. They decided to send riders north with one hundred head to the Gordon Strong Ranch and take the remainder north one hundred a week which would give Gordon time to get them all sold.

Twenty riders took one hundred head north as Dalton, Thunderchild and the remainder of the riders rode west to the village.

Chapter Twenty-Two

Back to the Village

"One hundred for the baby to make it an even five thousand."

It was almost four o'clock when Dalton and his riders reached the village. Raincloud reported that everything taken from the settlement and ranch was taken by pack horse to the top and waiting to be examined.

Their horses were taken away to the corrals for feed, water and a rub down. Wandering Buffalo told Dalton that the Chinese family were up top and doing fine. Dalton sniffed the air and could smell the steaks being cooked at the Forge.

"My God! Now I am really hungry!" Dalton exclaimed.

There was a roar of laughter as they all headed to the Forge. The women put the food out and everyone stopped talking. There were kegs of wine on the planks and as they left the table one by one, they told their stories about the raid over mugs of wine.

"When our riders get back from the Gordon Strong Ranch, we will have a feast!" Wandering Buffalo exclaimed.

Everyone lifted their mugs and shouted their approval.

"Are the builders back from Calgary?" Dalton asked.

"Yes. They are in the swimming pool with the Chinese. The Chinese love the hot water! I think we will have to fight to get them out!" Raincloud shouted.

Everyone had a good laugh.

"What about Anne and Sarah?" Dalton asked.

"They are in the Great Hall with the Chinese women and they are soaking in the hot water. Did you know Sarah is a hero" Wandering Buffalo said.

"She sure as hell is!"

After visiting for a while, just about everyone headed for the top.

When they got to the top, they all went to the pool to say Hello to the Chinese and then left in different direction. Some went into the Great Hall for more wine, some joined the Chinese in the pool and Dalton went to his lodge for a sleep.

Before noon the next day, the riders returned from the Gordon Strong Ranch. They reported to Dalton that the herd was delivered and Gordon said he could handle a hundred more every week.

"Gordon does not know if he should count all the money he is making or just weigh it" one of the riders said.

"That damn Gordon is getting rich but so are we!" Raincloud shouted.

"Tomorrow we will have a feast and a celebration so you fullas had better get some rest" Dalton said.

The riders left to visit and Dalton went with Raincloud to the Great Hall to examine everything taken in the massacre.

"Now, first of all, I would like to settle with the Chinese and find out what their plans are" Dalton said.

The four Chinese men were brought to the Great Hall to talk things over. Tom told the council that in China, there were also hot water pools hidden in the mountains. They all spoke about the hot water and how much they liked the caves and Great Hall.

"We would like to stay here and work but we are too young" Tom said.

The father spoke to Tom in Chinese.

"My father said he would like to stay here with my mother but this is a strange land and must keep the family together."

"It is best for your family to leave this place and become part of the new world" Beth said.

Tom nodded.

"How long did you work for McAllister?" Beth asked.

"Almost one year" Tom replied.

"And you were each promised one dollar a day for the seven of you" Beth stated.

"That is what my father told us."

"Now we are going to agree that the seven of you worked three hundred and fifty days. Seven dollars a day is not enough. The council wants you to have fourteen dollars a day."

"Holy! How much is that!" Tom exclaimed.

"Well, let me see." Beth paused to write down the numbers. "That comes to four thousand nine hundred dollars."

Tom jumped up and spoke in Chinese. The other three jumped up and they all spoke at once.

"It cannot be right! It is too much!" Tom exclaimed.

"One hundred for the baby and make it an even five thousand!" Raincloud shouted.

The council looked at Raincloud.

"One hundred for the baby and make it an even five thousand!" Dalton shouted.

Everyone laughed and agreed with the extra one hundred dollars. Tom stayed behind with his father as the other two went to tell the girls.

The five soon returned and there were tears of joy and hugs all around. Sarah saddled her horse and told the council she was going down to the Forge and would be back soon. The Chinese left and the council got back to business.

"Now, what about the Flatheads? I told their Chief I would send some money" Dalton stated.

"We have taken much money." Wandering Buffalo continued, "How about one thousand dollars?"

Dalton nodded his head and the council agreed.

"Give them half paper and the other half in silver dollars." Dalton continued, "Send for the scouts and take the Flatheads their money."

The scouts soon arrived and left for the Flathead nation with one thousand dollars in Yankee money. Five thousand dollars, in Canadian funds, was taken to Tom.

"We are running out of Canadian money. When the celebration is over, I will go to Calgary and exchange this

Yankee paper. I will also get the correct value for gold bricks" Dalton stated.

"What is next?" Dalton asked.

"I guess we have to figure out how much we will give the young riders who will be leaving after the feast and celebration" Beth stated.

"How many are there?" Dalton asked.

"Well, with the groomers, Sarah and four from the east, Anne, Big Man and assistants, dynamite assistants and the scouts there are twenty-three" Beth replied.

"Yes, and there is no need to count the dog warriors for we will divide up what is left over" Dalton added.

"So how much will we give the twenty-three riders?" Beth asked.

There was silence as the council waited for someone to speak.

"How much does two hundred dollars each come to?" Wandering Buffalo asked.

There was a short pause.

"Four thousand six hundred dollars" Beth answered.

"I think it is fair" Wandering Buffalo said.

Everyone agreed.

"Is there anything else to be paid?" Dalton asked.

"Not unless we owe Landsdown" Beth replied.

"Then put aside two thousand for Landsdown and tell us what it comes to" Dalton said.

"Twelve thousand six hundred dollars" Beth answered.

"How much more would it take to make twenty thousand dollars?"

Seven thousand four hundred dollars."

"Then put down seven thousand four hundred dollars for Chief Piapot. We will give him three thousand four hundred dollars this year and four thousand next year" Dalton said.

There were shouts of approval from the council.

"There is one other thing." Beth continued, "When you go to the bank with the Yankee money, they will want something for giving us Canadian dollars."

"I am not going to the bank. It is too risky so soon after the massacre. Vincent says Landsdown does much business with the Yankees and complains every day to his banker friends when they charge him for Yankee money.

He will be only too happy to take the Yankee money dollar for dollar" Dalton stated.

They all had a good laugh and agreed to come back at three o'clock.

On the way to his lodge, Sarah was returning from the Forge and stopped her horse in front of Dalton.

"When you get to counting the gold bricks, the McAllister documents will show that your council is a half brick short of a full load" Sarah said.

"How do you know?" Dalton said with an amused smile.

"Because I have it in my saddle bag."

Sarah dismounted and took the gold brick from her saddle bag.

"Jesus! How did you get that?"

"McAllister did not have a ring to offer when he proposed so we agreed on this half brick."

"Good Lord, girl! No wonder he was swearing at you!"

"So?"

"Well, I don't really know. He gave it to you as a gift long before the massacre so I do not think it has anything to do with the nation. A gift is a gift!"

"I do not want the nation to think I went into the Yankee Territory to get a gold brick" Sarah said.

"No one will think that" Dalton stated.

"Then I can keep it!"

"Well, not exactly." Dalton continued, "I do not want you wandering around with that gold brick and there is no need for anyone to know. I will sell it and give you the money."

"Good enough!"

Sarah laughed and gave Dalton the gold brick.

"Your grandmother has three hundred dollars waiting for you" Dalton smiled. "One hundred extra for leaving."

Sarah turned her horse and rode to the Great Hall. The Chinese men were back in the pool and when she walked into the women's lodge, the Chinese women told her about the five thousand dollars. They all had a good laugh about the one hundred dollars for the baby.

By three o'clock, the council returned to the Great Hall. Dalton wanted to know how much money and the value of the goods that were taken from the raid.

"We have not placed a value on sheets, blankets, canned goods, trunks, clothing, jewelry and these kinds of goods. They will be given as gifts, used by the nation or sent to the Trading Post." Beth continued, "Here is the value of what was taken."

Paper money	$56,200.00
Silver dollars	$10,000.00
Seven hundred sixty head of livestock	$45,600.00
Harness, saddles, bridals, wagons	$3,500.00
Rifles, handguns, ammunition, dynamite	$2,500.00
Five gold bricks	0

Nineteen gold half bricks..0
One Hundred thin gold plates....................................0

"This list will be the amount of money that the dog warriors and the women will divide. I have already deducted the twenty thousand dollar payout and the ten percent to Gordon for the livestock.

I did not include the gold because we do not know what the gold is worth. I think the bricks will be worth more per ounce than the nuggets we find in the streams.

Before the celebration, we will pay the young riders their two hundred dollars. We will give one hundred dollars to the dog warriors and the women if they need it. The remainder of the cash will be divided after the celebration when we convert both the gold and the Yankee cash into Canadian dollars.

Victoria and Wildfire are going to be busy at the Trading Post. They will be given a one third percentage of anything they sell that was taken from the massacre" Beth concluded.

The council agreed to discuss the documents after the feast.

Everyone praised Beth and were amazed at how much everything was worth. They discussed the gold and made small bets as to how much it was worth.

They left the warriors' room, locked the door and sat at tables in the dining room eating and drinking wine.

Dalton asked one of the girls about the feast. She assured Dalton that everything was being prepared and there was much food.

A young rider from the Yankee ranch came and reported to Dalton.

"Big Man is back from the Yankee ranch with the dead and wounded. They are at the Wandering Buffalo Lodge."

Raincloud and Dalton left with the rider to talk with Big Man. Beth, Sarah and grieving relatives were outside the Wandering Buffalo Lodge when they arrived.

"Where are the dead and wounded?" Dalton asked.

"They are inside the Forge. Big Man and his riders thought it would be best to talk over there" Beth said.

Wandering Buffalo walked to the Forge with Raincloud and Dalton. They went into the Forge and Dalton spoke with Big Man. The wounded were sitting at the large table eating soft biscuits and drinking wine. They were dog warriors and death was nothing new to them.

Dalton ordered Big Man and the young riders to go with the wounded to the top for food and rest. Raincloud and Dalton looked at the three dead warriors and left with Wandering Buffalo to talk with Beth.

"It looks like we have lost three dog warriors. Where will they be buried?" Dalton asked.

"Two in the ground and one in the trees" Beth replied.

"Are the families all here?" Raincloud asked.

"Yes!" Beth replied

"I will go with Raincloud and the family to put Lone Coyote in the trees. The rest of you can bury the other two" Dalton stated.

It was late in the afternoon before the burials were complete.

"Well, everyone is here except Gordon Strong and the warriors who took the cattle north" Beth said.

"Yes. They will probably be here in the morning." Dalton continued, "I want you to know that the nation is thankful for your prayers. It makes a difference."

Dalton spoke to the dead warriors families' and left with Raincloud for the top.

Chapter Twenty-Three

The Four Mile Race

"Great horse! Horse slip but win anyhow!"

The next morning, the scouts returned from the Flathead nation. Gordon and Heather arrived and Vincent was with them. Beth and Wandering Buffalo came by just as Gordon was putting two horses in the corral for feed and water.

"Are these the two winners?" Beth asked.

"They can run like the wind" Gordon replied.

"Maybe I will put a dollar or two on them. They are good looking horses" Wandering Buffalo said.

"I have a book and receipts for you, Chief Beth" Vincent stated.

Beth took a quick look at the book.

"It would appear as though Landsdown owes us some money."

"Yes. One thousand twenty-two dollars and seventy-five cents."

"Does Landsdown agree on the amount?"

"I don't know. I will let Chief Dalton talk to him" Vincent replied.

"What time do the races start?" Vincent asked.

"They start at two o'clock" Beth answered.

Vincent turned his horse and left for the top. He stopped at the garden and visited with the warriors and their wives as they dug and picked vegetables. Bags of vegetables were waiting to be picked up and large baskets were filled with raspberries, blueberries and berries from the trees.

When he reached the second level, Vincent put his horse in the corral and removed a pair of short pants from his saddle bag. He then left for the Great Hall on the third level to say Hello and get something to eat. Dalton and Raincloud invited him to sit down and one of the women brought him a plate of steak and fried potatoes. The three talked as they ate.

"How is everything at the Trading Post?" Dalton asked.

"There are new people arriving in Calgary every day and the Trading Post is busy. The Wildes are very pleased with the addition and I have money in my saddle bags to give you" Vincent reported.

"Are you ready for the pool?" Raincloud asked.

"You bet I am! I have my short pants right here! I saw the three Chinese men helping out with the tables. Where are the other four?"

"The two women are in the kitchen and we set up a table south of the pool overlooking the valley for the mother and father. They wanted to help but we talked them into just having a good rest before they leave. Sarah keeps taking them food and wine. They tell her she is Hero!" Dalton exclaimed.

There was laughter as Vincent left for the pool. On the way, he stopped to talk with Michael and Anne. Michael told Vincent he could use the hundred dollars he was keeping in Winnipeg.

"It is no problem." Vincent continued, "The nation owes me two hundred dollars. I will give you one hundred dollars and keep the money I put away for you. There is a little interest owing, maybe a dollar or two."

Michael and Anne continued their conversation as Vincent went to the warriors' small lodge, just south of the pool, to change into his short pants.

"What did he say when you told him?" Michael asked.

"Not much. He is going to Calgary and admitted to several relationships with other women. I asked him about Three Killers granddaughter and he told me she was already in Calgary."

"The nation will give us two hundred dollars each! That is enough to buy the ranch!" Michael exclaimed.

"I have some good news. I did not want to tell anybody about our plans but I did ask about the ranch and what would become of it. My mother mentioned it to your father and Chief Dalton just shrugged his shoulders and told my mother that when they raided the settlement, the nation got their money back.

I think we will get the ranch. It is in my name and the nation does not want to go into Yankee Territory again."

"Yes! I think you are right. If the nation tried to sell the ranch, it just might put the Yankees on our trail so why should they bother. It did not cost them a penny!" Michael exclaimed.

"I have to go to the Great Hall. My mother wants me to help get the tickets ready for the race."

Anne left for the women's lodge and Michael went to help with the tables.

As she went into the Great Hall, the kitchen was in an uproar. Instead of turning left into the women's lodge, Anne went to the kitchen area and asked what all the excitement was about.

"The Chinese girls have cleaned the fish so that it has no bones!" one of the women exclaimed.

"That is good but nothing to get excited about" Anne stated.

"That is not what excites us!"

"Then what is it?" Anne asked.

"They mix flour, baking powder, stirred in water, a little brown sugar and other things. Then they lay both sides of the fish on the mixture and put it into the boiling grease. When it comes out, it is golden brown and they sprinkle it with the dill, some pepper and some salt. It only takes a few minutes and it is delicious!"

Anne went over and one of the Chinese girls put a piece of the fish on a plate and sprinkled it with the dill, pepper and salt. Anne ate a mouthful and her eyes lit up.

"Good Lord! Do your men know how to do this?" Anne exclaimed.

"Oh, yes."

"I think you better get Tom and the other two up here! Everyone will want to try this!" Anne exclaimed.

"We can also do this with small pieces of chicken and cut potatoes can also be made brown in just minutes."

"What is your name?"

"My name is Lu."

"Well, Lu, you really started something. Your men will be here soon and our women will be anxious to help."

Anne took another piece of fish and went to the women's lodge.

In the pool, the riders were talking about the race.

"I hear you are riding for Gordon?" Raincloud asked.

"Yes. He said I could keep what he gets if his horses are winners. He just wants to watch them run and make a bet with the nation" Vincent replied.

"What races are you in?"

"The first and the fourth."

"Well, I will be riding against you in the fourth" Raincloud said.

"I will be betting on myself, Chief Raincloud."

"I will be betting on my horse!"

Raincloud got out of the pool and told Vincent he was going to the warriors' room to get a hundred dollars to make some bets and buy a little whiskey.

"All the young riders are getting their two hundred dollars" Raincloud said.

"Wait for me! I will go with you, Chief Raincloud."

When they reached the warriors' room, Dalton and a few of the women were paying out money. By noon, all the young riders were paid out and the dog warriors and women who needed money, took a hundred dollars. Their names were written on a piece of paper.

In the dining room, many had gathered to get a piece of fish. The Chinese were laughing as they cooked. The French women learned fast and could almost keep up with them. Fifty cents was charged for a plate of food.

On the second level, one of the caverns was set up for wine and whiskey at twenty-five cents for a mug of wine or a small glass of whiskey. There were also many baskets of soft biscuits and berries that were free.

When the tickets were ready, Anne, Beth and Sarah took them to the large cavern on the second level where the wine and whiskey was sold. Four of the young riders moved a long counter to the front of the cavern. Signs were hung above the counter to explain the racing and betting rules.

Rules

1. Start and finish line on lower level.
2. Each rider must stop for ten minutes at two mile station.
3. Each rider must report to time keepers at two mile station.
4. Timekeepers will tell each rider when to leave.
5. Any rider who leaves without being told by the timekeeper will finish last.

Winning rider................................Five dollars
Losing riders................................One dollar

6. Riders paid by nation.
7. Six riders each race.

Betting

1. Price of ticket................................Two dollars each
2. Limit of two tickets
3. You must have ticket to collect

4. Nation................................Ten percent of money bet
5. Remainder of money................Divided by winning
                                                  tickets

How you Win

Number of winning tickets Twenty
Total money bet................................$400.00
Ten percent to nation........................$40.00
Total money remaining.....................$360.00
Each ticket:................................360 ÷ 20 = $18.00

Time

1. Four races................................One hour apart
2. First race................................Two o'clock

The last sign that was hung up names the six riders and their horses for each of the four races. After a quick look at the sign, the betting soon began. To make sure everyone got a chance to bet, tickets were sold one race at a time. Ticket sales for the first race would stop five minutes before starting time and the number of the last ticket sold was posted on the board. The ticket counter would stay open and tickets for the second race could be purchased up to five minutes before starting time. Again, the number of the last ticket sold would be posted before starting time. The same procedure would apply for the third and fourth race.

Before each race was over, Anne and Beth could count the tickets sold and the money. The amount of money a ticket would pay was posted on the board beside the name of the rider and horse.

The dining room in the Great Hall was almost empty so the workers went down to make their bets. Tom told his brother and brother-in-law that for twelve dollars, they could bet each horse.

"What if the horse that wins does not pay us much?" Tom's brother asked.

"Then we lose a few dollars" Tom replied.

"I do not like it. I will buy a ticket on two horses that I like" Tom's brother stated.

"Me too" the brother-in-law added.

The women also wanted to pick their own horses.

It was almost time for the first race and a crowd gathered at the finish line while others watched from the upper levels. The riders and their horses were called to the start line. A blast was heard from an old musket and the horses leaped forward.

The six horses galloped west beside a large slough that turned south to the first station marking the route. The horses had to turn south and around four judges before turning north to the ten minute stop station.

Two young riders turned south near the edge of the slough to cut off distance and their horses slipped in the mud. One horse went down and the rider was thrown into the water. The second horse slipped and stumbled but made it back up to the grass. Two judges rode out from the station. One judge caught the horse and the other one went to the slough.

"Are you all right?"

"Yes, I am fine" the rider continued. I guess it is now a five horse race."

"Probably four" the judge stated.

The rider's horse was not hurt so the three rode back to the first station.

The crowd cheered when they saw the downed rider get back on his horse. The five horses made the turn north around the first station and opened up as they ran for the ten minute station. The fifth horse that slipped in the mud was running last.

As the horses neared the ten minute stop station, they had to run up a steep hill.

"Where are my horses?!" Tom's wife shouted.

"I will go to the trunk and get the glasses" Tom shouted.

Everyone was cheering and shouting as the horses flew across the meadow. One horse was crowded out as the two horses up front made a turn for the hill.

Tom returned with the glasses and gave them to his wife.

"Yes! That is my horse! The red and white one that slip in the mud! He is closer now!"

"But still last!" Tom continued, "What is your other horse?"

"I only bet one. I bet two tickets on red and white one. I see his number. He is number four."

The rider in fourth place took his horse to a ravine but there were too many trees and turned around. Number four and the horse that was crowded out were almost tied for third. The two horses up front reached the steep hill and one of them balked half way up and was last going up the hill.

When the first horse reached the top, a judge took the reins and the rider ran to the time keeper.

"Your time is two zero eight. You will leave at two eighteen."

Back at the counter, the calculations were completed and the payout for each horse was posted.

"Oh Lordy! Everyone in the village must have bet! There is eight hundred and forty dollars here!" Beth exclaimed.

"Well mother, you wanted the church and cottage for Reverend Stonebreaker!" Anne shouted.

At the ten minute station, the horses were lined up one after the other according to their time. The first rider was told to go and the other four soon followed. Two of the front runners would not open up on the steep downhill and the order changed. The first horse was still in front but number four was close behind.

By the time they reached the meadow, number four was almost beside the front runner. With less than a mile to go, the front runner began to creep ahead. The horses could now be seen without glasses and Tom's wife shouted for her horse to go faster.

Dalton and Raincloud, who were close by, walked over and Raincloud told her not to worry.

"He will win?!" she asked.

"Yes" Dalton answered.

"How? He has made more space!" she exclaimed.

"My son, Michael, is riding your horse. He is a buffalo horse and belongs to Michael. In just a few seconds, the horses have to run up the slope to the finish line. The slope is where your number four horse will beat the long legs they call Spider" Dalton explained.

With less than a quarter mile to the finish line, number four chewed up the ground. He ran past the finish line two lengths ahead of the horse they called Spider.

Tom's wife jumped in the air and gave hugs all around. Dalton went to the counter to see how much they won. When he returned, even Dalton was excited.

"Our horse was not a favorite! We won sixteen dollars and fifty cents on each ticket!" Dalton exclaimed.

"Holy! I have two tickets! Let me see . . ."

"You have both won thirty-three dollars!" Tom exclaimed.

Dalton and the Chinese went to the counter to get their money.

Michael took the saddle off his horse and removed the bridal. After putting on the halter, Michael took his horse for a victory walk to collect his money. Everyone told Michael what a good rider he was and had much praise for his horse. Dalton was proud of his son and told him so.

Tom's wife put her arms around the horse's neck and gave Michael a hug as he stopped to talk.

"Great horse! Horse slip but win anyhow!"

Michael laughed and went to the counter.

"You came close, Gordon" Dalton said.

"I knew we needed a bigger lead going up the slope if a buffalo horse was chasing us" Gordon stated.

"Vincent rode a good race."

"He sure did. He got as much out of the horse as he could."

"Did you taste the fish dipped in the oil?" Dalton asked.

"Delicious! Heather is up helping in the kitchen. She will know how to do it before we leave."

Dalton made a bet on the second race and went back to his job of selling whiskey and wine. The racing continued during the day with heavy betting and celebrating. Vincent won the fourth race and took forever doing his victory walk.

After paying the riders, the nation made two hundred and seventy dollars for the church and cottage. Dalton gave Beth two hundred and ten dollars from the whiskey and wine sales. The whiskey and wine sales moved to the Great Hall.

"We have done good, Chief Dalton, almost five hundred dollars and there will be much more from the kitchen" Beth stated.

Towards evening, the celebrations got under way. Fires were started everywhere. There was a big fire down by the finish line with drums and much dancing.

On the planks in front of the caverns, violins, guitars and drums sounded as the step dancers showed their stuff. The riders got out of the pool and went into the dining room for food and drinks.

In the morning, people were not moving in numbers before noon. Everyone spoke of the wonderful time they had. They spoke most about the horse race and asked Dalton to have one every August. Dalton was in agreement and said he would speak with the council.

Dalton sent for Benjamin and the builders he sent to Calgary. They soon joined Dalton and Beth in the dining room for food and drinks.

"I would like you and the builders to make the Forge into a church and the Wandering Buffalo Lodge into a summer house for Reverend David Stonebreaker and his family" Dalton stated.

"Two of the builders I sent have jobs in Calgary. The rest of us can stay. Some of the dog warriors know how to build and with their help, we will have the church and summer house ready in no time" Benjamin said.

"Good! Now we are going to pay you and your men three dollars a day because you could be making money somewhere else. You do not have to pay for anything! You can send for your family and we will pay for that too" Dalton said.

Benjamin told Dalton it would go faster if the Wandering Buffalo Lodge was torn down and the lumber cleaned. Dalton agreed as it would give the dog warriors something to do while the Forge was being finished.

As the Strong family and Vincent were getting ready to leave, Dalton dropped by to speak to Vincent.

"I would like you to stay in Calgary for a few more days until we get this Yankee money and the gold turned into Canadian dollars" Dalton stated.

"Do you want me to approach Landsdown?"

"Yes" Dalton continued. "Do not speak to Landsdown about the gold. Just kinda ask around out of curiosity. The bankers will know what a brick of gold is worth but they do not have to know we have some."

"I understand" Vincent said.

"Oh! And good riding" Dalton added.

Vincent smiled and left with the Gordon Strong family.

Dalton walked over to where Thunderchild and two of the builders were hooking up the one wagon and the buggy. Several of the women were talking to the Chinese family. There were tears and hugs as the family climbed into the wagon and buggy.

Beth gave Thunderchild and the two builders twenty dollars each for travel money. They told Beth they still had over two hundred dollars each but she made them take it.

"The next time you see me, I will not be in the shacks, Chief Dalton. Coming here to help out was just what I needed" Thunderchild said.

Dalton nodded and thanked the three for coming.

"Goodbye, Hero!" Tom shouted to Sarah.

Late in the afternoon, just about all the young people left the village. From a distance, Dalton saw Big Man saying Goodbye and was surprised when he rode north alone.

It was not long before Michael and Anne approached Dalton. They told him their plans and Dalton did not have anything to say. Dalton liked Big Man for he was one of six boys who helped him kill eight renegades.

"The ranch is in my name and I guess we would like to know where we stand. The nation did get their money back for the purchase."

"Yes. It is true that the ranch did not cost the nation any money but it did cost someone money."

"Who?" Michael asked.

"Mr. and Mrs. Wilson" Dalton replied.

"But they are gone!" Anne exclaimed.

"I know where they are. The Chinese told me" Dalton stated.

"So you want us to pay the Wilsons" Michael stated.

"Yes" Dalton answered.

"What if the council says we do not have to pay?" Anne asked.

"I will say No to the council."

"How much do you want us to pay?" Michael asked.

"Four hundred dollars. There is a council meeting tomorrow morning and you both can attend."

Dalton left to speak with Beth, Sarah and Wandering Buffalo. He told them what his position was regarding the ranch.

"They will get one hundred dollars each like everyone else gets when they leave. They also got two hundred dollars each for going into the Yankee Territory. That is six hundred dollars and they have a little more money besides" Wandering Buffalo stated.

"Yes. No one else got anything for nothing and I am sure the Wilson family could use the money" Beth added.

Beth and Wandering Buffalo told Dalton they were going to the little white church in two days.

"I think Michael and Anne are coming with us" Beth said.

"And I am going too" Sarah continued. "You and Louise should come.

"We will be ready."

Chapter Twenty-Four

The Wilson Ranch

"They have a very strange Chief. He thinks friendship is better than money."

In the morning, Michael and Anne attended the council meeting and Beth gave a report on the Wilson ranch.

"Even though the nation recovered the four hundred dollars paid out for the Wilson ranch, the ranch could never have been purchased without nation money. The council has decided that it is fair to pay the Wilsons for the money they paid out for the land and buildings.

Now the council has some good news. After looking at the documents, we find that the Wilsons paid three hundred dollars for the land and they borrowed two hundred dollars from McAllister to put up buildings and buy cattle from him.

However, they only paid back eighty dollars. Chief Dalton found out in Cut Bank that McAllister's favorite trick was to tear down fences, steal the livestock and blame it on the Flatheads. This is probably what happened to the Wilsons.

The council agreed to a new price of three hundred and eighty dollars for the ranch. The nation will make sure the Wilsons get the money. That is our decision."

"We have agreed that the Wilsons should get the money they paid for the ranch and buildings. If they did not get paid, it would make us just like McAllister." Michael continued, "Three hundred and eighty dollars is a good surprise."

Anne gave her mother the three hundred and eighty dollars. Michael and Anne visited for a while before leaving the warriors' lodge.

"Now, Theresa Lone Coyote and several other dog warriors have a question or two for the council. Theresa?"

"Yes. I am told that because my husband died in the raid, I will get his money that is to be divided. I will have maybe two thousand dollars. I do not need hardly any of it for everything is here. Why did the council not give more to the young people we put on the plains?" Theresa asked.

"That is a good question. I do not have the answer for you but maybe Chief Dalton can answer" Beth stated.

Dalton got to his feet.

"This village is part of the Assiniboine nation. I am Chief of Chiefs in this village and Chief Piapot is Chief of the Assiniboine Nation. It was Chief Piapot's decision to put our young people on the plains with papers, land and enough money to get a start.

When this was done, all the money left in the village was to be divided equally among every woman and man over fifty-five years who are from this village. This will be done and I will tell you why.

On the reserves, there are certain things which the nations are entitled to by the treaties they have signed. These are things that do not concern us.

With the young people we have put into the white man's world, there are no entitlements. They will not be able to walk into a bank and borrow money for even though they have papers, they will be treated like Indians. Until this changes, we are the banks.

If one of my children or grandchildren need a little help to carry on, I will help them if they are trying. If they do not try, I will make sure they get food and that is all. This is what I will do and everyone else can do as they please."

There was laughter and much praise for Dalton.

"Now, since the raid, several of you have come to me with concern about the money you receive and have asked the council to keep it for you. I have spoken to the council and this we will not do" Beth said.

"It has been said that you get smarter as you get older but this is not always true. I have seen it when the older you get the more stupid you get. Already I am starting to feel like this." There was a roar of laughter and when everyone settled down, the dog warrior continued. "I agree with Chief Dalton. There will be those who will come and ask for money but do not deserve any. I think it will be hard to say No."

The council was silent for they knew he was right and some kind of help should be offered.

"You are right! There is reason for concern. Come back at two o'clock and we will have an answer for everyone including me" Dalton stated.

When Dalton left the warriors' lodge, he went to talk with Michael and Anne.

"Well, how is the money adding up?" Dalton asked.

"Pretty good!" Anne continued, "We had two hundred dollars each for our part in the raid, another one hundred dollars each for leaving the village, I had saved one hundred and fifty dollars and Michael got his one hundred dollars from Vincent. After giving the nation three hundred and eighty dollars, we have four hundred and seventy dollars."

"Do not forget! I won thirty-five dollars in the race" Michael added.

"Yes, and I bought two tickets on Thunder so counting the winnings, we have about five hundred and thirty dollars left over" Anne stated.

Dalton smiled. I can see that you both are excited. You should have enough money to get off to a good start."

"Yes. The only big expense will be money for cattle and horses" Michael said.

"You should not have to pay anything for cattle and horses. Anne has her horse and you have Thunder. Also, you have two horses in my herd."

"Why do we not have to pay for cattle?" Anne asked.

"The riders told me that around twenty or fifty head of cattle were left behind. Tomorrow we will load your other two horses with supplies and you both can go from the church to the ranch. If you go through the Flathead nation, their Chief will give you a few riders to help out with the cattle."

"How much will that cost?" Michael asked.

"Probably nothing for they have a very strange Chief. He thinks that friendship is better than money."

"We will give the riders something. Without having to buy livestock, we have good money" Anne said.

Dalton nodded and left to drink wine with Raincloud.

At two o'clock, the council returned to the warriors' room and Beth spoke to the large crowd.

"The council has decided that your money should be deposited in the bank. It can be arranged so that it will take one other signature for you to take money out. You can choose a member of the council or any other person you trust. You can change this at any time.

Now, just so you do not have to travel to a bank if you want money, the council will always have money on hand for you. You will sign a bank slip for the money you receive.

It would be a good idea to have five or ten dollars in your lodge. If someone wants to borrow more than five or ten dollars, they must come with you to a council meeting. The council will know if they have a good reason to borrow or if they just want to spend your money to have a good time. You will be advised and you will decide. I do not think that very many liars will show up at a council meeting.

Also, there is a thing called a Will. This paper names the people who get your money and what you own when you die. The council can help you with this paper. The Will can be changed at any time and only your Last Will is of value. You do not have to give everything to just one person. This Will can be left with a bank, lawyer or with anyone else that you trust. A member of the council will witness your Will."

There were a few questions but everyone was pleased with what Beth had to say. Just about everyone wanted to get started on their Will. Beth told everyone about the marriages at the little white church and appointed several assistants to help out while she was gone.

The wedding party left for the dining area and they were joined by Raincloud.

"I guess Isabelle would like to get married" Raincloud said.

There was a moment of silence before everyone began talking at once. They all congratulated Raincloud on his decision.

"This is going to be so much fun!" Sarah exclaimed.

"Do not worry about supplies for the trip" Dalton continued. "Just bring your good cloth for the pictures!"

"What time do we leave?" Raincloud asked.

"We will meet here for breakfast and leave before ten o'clock. Mr. and Mrs. Ranier! How nice!" Beth exclaimed.

Raincloud visited for a while before leaving to get his good cloth ready.

Early the next morning, the wedding party got off to a good start. Dalton stopped at the Forge to have a few words with Benjamin Stonebreaker.

"How is everything going, Benjamin?" Dalton asked.

"As you can see, we have lots of help and we will be done here shortly after you get back" Benjamin replied.

"One of the boys from the Gordon Strong Ranch will bring a telegram from Vincent." Dalton continued,

"Have Gordon send Vincent a telegram telling him to meet me at the ranch."

Benjamin nodded and the wedding party left for the little white church.

About an hour from the church, Dalton and Raincloud rode ahead to meet with Father Dupuis. By the time they reached the church, it was clouding up and looking like rain.

"Welcome! Welcome!" Father Dupuis exclaimed.

"We have brought a party of three to get married. This is Raincloud and he is one of the three" Dalton said.

"This is marvelous!" Father Dupuis continued, "It is starting to rain but not to worry. After the ceremony, we can celebrate in the cabin.

"We have brought much food and wine. We have even brought a small keg for you" Raincloud said.

"Raspberry?"

"Of course!" Dalton shouted.

"And we have enough deer steaks for everyone" Raincloud added.

"I will have Tom start the fires in the cook stove."

The rest of the wedding party soon arrived and went to the barn where Dalton and Raincloud were waiting.

"Sarah and Louise will help me with the horses. The rest of you happy brides and grooms had better head to the church and get ready" Dalton said.

Dalton led the three supply horses to the cabin and Tom helped him unload. Dalton gave Tom thirty dollars.

"Father Dupuis thinks I give him too much money. You can give him the thirty dollars when we leave."

"The French girls from your settlement have showed me how to make soft biscuits and pie. I will get started right away so we can have biscuits and wine while we wait for the steaks. The pies will be ready for dessert" Tom said with a smile.

Dalton nodded and led the supply horses back to the barn for feed and water. When they were done, Dalton and the girls left for the church. The brides and grooms stood across from one another in their good cloth and made their vows. When it was over, there were hugs, kisses and tears. Everyone admired the rings which were made in the small Forge.

After the pictures, the wedding party left for the cabin. Tom had two kegs of wine set up and everyone helped themselves to soft biscuits. Dalton watched as Sarah went outside with her mug and a soft biscuit. Dalton went out to join her.

"Well, what do you think?" Dalton asked.

"I will not tell you a lie, Chief Dalton. In a way, I wish it were my mother and father who got married" Sarah said.

"I know" Dalton said.

"When I get back to Calgary, I will see how he is making out. I hope he finds what he is looking for" Sarah said.

"Vincent says there is a place in Winnipeg that encourages people like your father to come and learn about the white man's medicine. If your father wants to go, the nation will make sure he has the money" Dalton stated.

"It is good to know that the nation cares about my father."

"And the nation cares about you too, Sarah. When you leave the village and get paid for the gold, you will have enough money to get a good start. Do not be foolish with your money" Dalton stated.

"Don't worry, Chief Dalton. I already know what happens to people who throw their money around."

"Good."

"You know, I have been meaning to ask you a question."

"What is it?" Dalton asked.

"Why were you and Chief Raincloud laughing so hard when McAllister was calling me all those filthy names?"

Dalton started to laugh and Sarah gave him a mean look.

"Well, we thought it was funny because he was making it so clear that he did not love you anymore and we just kept wondering what filthy name he would call you next."

Dalton started to laugh again and could not stop.

"Jesus! You and that Chief Raincloud make a marvelous pair!"

Sarah went inside and left Dalton on the veranda laughing by himself.

After supper, Father Tom brought out his violin and Michael went for his guitar. Father Tom and Isabelle took turns playing the violin as the wedding party danced to the music. Everyone laughed and cheered when Father Dupuis and Father Tom took to the floor and showed their steps.

It was late in the evening before the party started to wind down. Some went to the loft to sleep and some went to the church. Sarah fell asleep on the couch.

In the morning, the newlyweds thanked Father Dupuis for the pictures and a wonderful party. When they all left, Tom gave Father Dupuis the thirty dollars.

"Where do they get it!?"

After riding for close to an hour, Michael and Anne rode south to their ranch and the rest of the wedding party rode north to the village.

Chapter Twenty-Five

Half Brick Short of a Full Load

"These reserves are just glorified concentration camps."

It was early in the afternoon when they reached the village. The warriors greeted the newlyweds by their married names. There was much laughter and story telling. Benjamin gave Dalton a letter from Vincent and the wedding party left for the upper levels.

"We will meet at four o'clock in the warriors' room to discuss the prices Vincent has sent" Dalton stated.

After taking care of their horses, the wedding party went to their lodges. Sarah went to the Great Hall.

When Dalton walked into the warriors' room, everyone was seated at the long table. Dalton gave Beth the letter from Vincent which she read to the council.

ATTENTION:

Yankee moneyDollar for Dollar

Gold (value)$21.00 per ounce

Gold (offered)$14.00 per ounce

Two-thirds of the value is a good deal. I will remain at the Gordon Strong Ranch until you come.

"Did anyone here expect full value for the gold?" Dalton asked.

They all shook their heads and said No.

"It looks as though we will get two-thirds." Beth continued, "I think it is a good deal."

The council all agreed.

So far as the gold is concerned, there is nothing left to discuss. We will now burn all the documents that point to gold or cash" Dalton said.

Beth held the documents and rose to speak but Dalton stopped her.

"That's right. Just bring them over here."

Beth took the documents to the fireplace and gave them to Dalton.

"I just took a look at the documents. We are short one half brick of gold" Beth whispered.

"I know. I will tell you about it later" Dalton said with a smile.

Dalton lit the documents on fire and put them in the fireplace. When the documents finished burning, Dalton and Beth returned to the long table.

"Now there is one thing about the gold to consider. The gold small plates have ten ounces and twenty-four karats stamped on them. Now I just want to make it clear that, according to Vincent, the plates are worth two hundred and ten dollars. If anyone is interested, you can buy a gold plate for one hundred and forty dollars because that is all we will get for one plate" Dalton continued.

"Who knows! The white man is crazy for gold! Maybe it will go up in price. Beth will leave a piece of paper in the dining room to write your name so we can take the money from your share. One plate per person unless there are plates left over. Once everyone has a chance, then you can buy as many plates as you want. We will meet here again at seven o'clock.

All the gold plates were sold before six o'clock. Because of the demand, some of the plates were reduced from each person to each lodge before the rest were sold.

When everyone returned at seven, Beth and her assistants showed the council a new chart and a total of the money to be divided.

Total Money

Previous money without gold	$117,800.00
Five gold bricks (2,192 oz x $14.00)	30,688.00
Nineteen half bricks (4164.8 oz x $14.00)	58,307.02
One hundred gold plates (1000 oz x $14.00)	14,000.00
	$220,795.02

Each person (220,795.00 divided by 193) $1,144.00
Those who bought gold plates will receive$140.00 less.

"Now there may be money coming in from Landsdown and other small amounts" Beth continued.

"The village will keep this money on hand to maintain the church, to cover your bank withdrawal slips and any other small items."

"Is there anything else?" Dalton asked.

"We are now on our own. When this money is gone, we will be poor and when the village runs out of money, what will become of us?" an old warrior asked.

"There is no reason for you or the village to run out of money. Behind the kitchen, there are shelves that still have many jars of food from last year and in the valley we have buffalo, cattle and horses. The herds are strong and increase each year. Now that we are less than two hundred, the village can sell a few" Dalton continued. "No one in the village has to pay for food. The warriors' room that we stand in will be divided and part of it will be a store. You will be able to buy whatever you need to make buckskin and the white man's cloth. It will also have many other things for our needs. The store will sell to you for a little more and make some money.

Whatever you make that is for sale, the village will have it taken to the Calgary Trading Post and you will get good money for what you make.

Every fall, the garden gives us more than we can use. What we sell will be divided. Also, I for one, will continue to pan for gold and add to the money I have.

So enjoy life! Eat as much as you want and soak in the hot pool."

Everyone had a good laugh and the council agreed to consider the remainder of the documents after the gold was sold. Before leaving the warriors' room, Dalton asked Beth to join him.

"You are correct about the missing half brick" Dalton continued. "I have the half brick. I will sell it on the side and give the money to your granddaughter and no one has to know."

"Sarah!?"

"Yes. The half brick belongs to her and not the village."

"Why?"

Dalton told Beth how Sarah came by the brick. Beth was silent and then agreed with Dalton.

"Good Lord! That girl has more money coming than either of us!" Beth exclaimed.

"Almost three times as much. Three thousand, sixty-eight dollars and eight cents is what she has coming" Dalton added.

Beth was shaking her head and Dalton was laughing as they left the warriors' room.

The next morning, ten small suitcases were brought to the warriors' room and each suitcase was filled with about forty-five pounds of gold wrapped in cloth. The suitcases were then stuffed with clothes. Ten riders took them below where a wagon was waiting.

"Chief Raincloud will take three riders and ride the trail ahead. Sarah and the three of us will ride behind the wagon. You two will ride to the ranch and tell Vincent to take the six o'clock to Calgary and have a buggy waiting for us in the morning."

Just before twelve o'clock, the riders and wagon reached the Gordon Strong Ranch. The two groomers unsaddled the horses and took them to the corral for feed and water. The two drivers took the wagon into the barn and stayed with the gold.

Gordon met the riders on the veranda and took them inside for dinner. Heather and her two daughters gave each of them a hug and put the food on the table.

"Vincent said you should not bunch up when you take the morning train" Gordon said.

"Vincent is right" Dalton agreed.

"Our suitcases are black and brown but all the same. Do you have any small suitcases?" Raincloud asked.

"I believe we have four or five we could throw into the mix" Gordon answered.

The first two who got up from the table went to the barn and sent the drivers in for dinner. Gordon put a keg of wine out on the veranda and Sarah brought soft biscuits.

"I have some good news. A big stockyard operation has been built close to Calgary in a place they call Ogden. These people have contacted me and want me to send them some cattle." Gordon continued, "I have put through about two hundred head of your herd. How many head do you think are left?"

"About six hundred" Raincloud replied.

"Bring two hundred at a time two days apart and I will have all your money for you in less than ten days."

The riders shouted their approval and filled up their mugs.

Early in the morning, Dalton thanked Heather for the suitcases and the ten riders left in two buggies for Lethbridge. The station was not that busy when they arrived. They went into the station one at a time and did not bunch up. When they boarded the train, they sat in separate seats.

Vincent was waiting with the buggy when they arrived.

In Calgary, after putting the luggage in the buggy, eight of the riders went into the station and purchased tickets to Lethbridge. Vincent, Dalton and Sarah took the road east to the Trading Post.

Victoria and Wildfire were waiting for them on the planks. After the suitcases were taken into the small bedroom, they sat around the big kitchen table catching up with the news and drinking coffee.

272 / Chapter Twenty-Five

"Where is Timothy and the girls?" Dalton asked.

"They went with Helen to the ranch and we will follow Vincent to Calgary. I knew you would like a little privacy for your meeting with Landsdown. Nobody comes here after four o'clock" Victoria stated.

"We lit the fires in the bathroom. Let me show you and Sarah how everything works" Wildfire said.

"Great idea!" Dalton exclaimed.

Dalton and Sarah were very impressed and returned to the big room to buy some clothes. Victoria and Wildfire did not want them to pay but Dalton insisted.

"There is soap in both rooms and bubble bath for the tub" Victoria added as she left to join Wildfire.

"I will be back before five o'clock with Landsdown and his business partner. They are going to half the gold." Vincent continued, "If they purchase the bricks, how much do you think the village has coming?"

"One hundred two thousand, nine hundred ninety-five dollars" Dalton replied.

"You are out by two cents!" Vincent shouted.

The two wagons left and Dalton took care of the store while Sarah soaked in the tub.

It was almost five o'clock when they were finished cleaning up. Dalton poured two mugs of wine and they went out to the veranda to wait for the buggy.

"I just love the bathrooms." Sarah continued, "It is so nice and warm in there with the two fireplaces going!"

"Yes, and to think that we have enjoyed the village hot pools and baths for fifteen years."

"I know. That is the one thing about the village I will never forget!" Sarah exclaimed.

Before long, the buggy could be seen coming up the road. Sarah went inside to clean the kitchen table and put out five fancy wine glasses and five small whiskey glasses upside down on a tray. Dalton placed one full brick and one half brick of gold on the table.

Vincent brought his passengers inside. Landsdown was carrying two black suitcases and his partner a small box which he placed on the table. Landsdown put down his suitcases and walked directly over to Sarah and gave her a very enthusiastic hug.

"Good Lord, girl! Where have you been?" Landsdown asked.

"Visiting my mother and father" Sarah replied.

"Now, Sam, I would like you to meet Sarah Walker, the most beautiful girl in the west!" Landsdown exclaimed.

"She most certainly is!" Sam agreed and kissed the back of Sarah's hand.

"Now Mr. Dillon, I would like you to meet Sam Rosen. Sam, this is Joseph Dillon. Joseph is a friend of mine and a man of his word!"

The two shook hands and Dalton invited them to sit at the table.

"We have put out some glasses just in case we make a deal" Dalton stated.

"We always make a deal, Mr. Dillon!" Landsdown shouted.

Everyone had a good laugh. Dalton put the gold bricks in front of Landsdown and Sam opened up the small box. He proceeded to explain how he would test the gold.

"Now this brick is supposed to weigh twenty-seven point four pounds and the kt stands for karate. The brick is stamped 24 kt which means it is pure gold. We shall see."

Sam pulled a few metal pieces out of his box and made a small scale. He weighed both bricks and gave Landsdown a nod. He fooled around with a few more small tools before starting a gas fire inside a small round container.

After heating a corner of the bricks, he hit the corners with a small silver hammer. The corner of the bricks flattened out and Sam looked at Landsdown and nodded.

"I'll buy half" Sam stated.

"Good enough for me" Landsdown agreed.

Landsdown and Sam inspected the remaining bricks while Dalton and Vincent counted the money. Each side was satisfied and Sarah filled up the glasses. They all stood up, put their glasses together and shot back the whiskey.

As they sipped on their wine, Dalton told Landsdown that Sarah wanted to sell her half brick for the same price. Landsdown put some figures on a piece of paper and came up with three thousand sixty-eight dollars and eighty cents. Dalton and Sarah agreed that the price was correct.

"Now there is no problem here. I will buy the half brick but I do not think you should walk into the bank with this kind of money. I will take the brick and tomorrow I will give you a bank draft for the money. I will mark it as payment for materials. The draft is like cash and no one will ask questions. Is this satisfactory Sarah?" Landsdown asked.

"Very!" Sarah answered.

"Now Joseph, we are not yet out the door with the gold. I want you to know that we are making a great deal of money for doing very little. Do you feel this transaction is fair?"

"It is a good deal for both of us John" Dalton stated.

"The hotel reserves accommodations for me on a daily basis. When we get to Calgary, I will take you to your suite and carry on to my office. The suite and dinner at seven o'clock is on us!" Landsdown exclaimed.

"I do not think we will go anywhere without the money" Dalton stated.

"Of course not! We are going to order up room service!" Sam shouted.

The suitcases were put in the buggy and they headed down the road to Calgary.

When they reached the hotel, Landsdown went to the front desk for the key and gave it to Dalton.

"See you at seven o'clock."

That evening, Dalton had a new food experience of lemon pie topped with something fluffy and sweet. Sam commented on the raspberry wine and Dalton told him he would deliver a small keg to Landsdown as a gift.

As the dinner party broke up, Sam shook hands with everybody and Landsdown said he would attend to the bank drafts in the morning. They agreed to meet in the suite for breakfast shortly after ten o'clock.

Chapter Twenty-Six

Landsdown Unplugged

"What makes you think my name is Dalton?"

Shortly after ten o'clock the next morning, Landsdown arrived at the suite.

"I told them downstairs we were ready for breakfast."

"This is some hotel! About five people came at eight o'clock and cleaned the entire suite!" Dalton exclaimed.

"Nothing but the best for my friends."

Vincent heard a knock and opened the door. In came half the kitchen with square and round silver trays covered with silver lids. Five large plates along with cutlery were placed at one end of the long table and a huge silver coffee pot with a tap at the bottom was placed at the other end.

Two of the waiters replaced the table cloth and put a silver bowl of fruit in the center.

"Matilda will remain to make sure you have everything you need" the head waiter said.

When they left, Matilda went behind the long narrow table and lit the candles that were under the silver trays. She then brought two small silver bowls and placed them on the table. One was filled with sugar and the other one with cream. After setting four places of cutlery complete with cloth napkins, she brought four cupfuls of hot coffee to the table.

Matilda walked back behind the long narrow table and removed the lids from the silver trays.

"Well! Let's dig in!" Landsdown shouted.

Sarah went first and Matilda gave them their choice of bacon, sausage, steak, eggs, fried potatoes, pancakes with syrup and butter, toast and toast with cinnamon.

Another waiter soon appeared to take away plates from the table and pour more coffee. Dalton and Vincent went back for more one time and Landsdown went back twice.

When Landsdown stopped going back for more, five of the kitchen cleared everything that came from the kitchen except four clean cups, coffee pot and what was left of the food.

Everyone thanked the kitchen staff and praised Landsdown for the breakfast. He spoke with Sarah and handed her an envelope.

"Your draft is inside."

"Oh, thank you" Sarah said.

Sarah slipped on a light jacket and left to make a bank deposit. Vincent poured coffee and the three sat around laughing and discussing all their business deals.

Vincent finished his coffee and before leaving, he spoke to Dalton.

"I am going to find Sarah and say Goodbye to a few friends. I will bring the buggy here at about twelve thirty in time for you to catch the one o'clock south. I will be taking the two o'clock east" Vincent said.

Vincent shook hands with Landsdown and went to find Sarah.

"I sure have enjoyed his company!" Landsdown continued. "Vincent has a job with me any time he wants one!"

"I guess this wraps up just about all our business John. Mr. Wilde said you were a fair man to deal with and I agree with him" Dalton stated.

"Now I am going to tell you how I feel about the west and the rest of the country when it comes to Indians.

These reserves are just glorified concentration camps. Stay on your reserve! Keep the peace and we will give you rations! Could it be any worse!?

Every time I sit down with Government people, I tell them to give the Indians land and houses in the towns and let them have equal rights so they can grow with the nation. I even told them that in the far north, they should have their own country.

The entire world is moving ahead at a very fast pace and the people on these reserves are going nowhere and that is the same thing as going backwards. It will take the Indians hundreds of years to dig their way out of the graves they have been put into at the end of a gun.

The Government is not going to listen to me. They like it just the way it is. I hope the Indians all find gold bricks and large amounts of cash floating in their streams just like your people did!" Landsdown shouted.

Dalton could not hold back his laughter. When he was finished laughing, Landsdown continued.

"Now when you came to me with money saying you wanted to free eight hundred Indians and put them on the plains with equal rights, I was pleased to be a part of it. Their contribution to this nation will be soon in coming.

Your Chief Piapot deserves a great deal of credit for the manner in which he has gone about his business and so do you Chief Dalton."

Dalton's eyes widened and there was a few seconds of silence.

"Chief Dalton?"

"Yes. You represent a nation of people and that is what chiefs do."

"What makes you think my name is Dalton?"

"I spent a little time east of here and I met a U.S. Marshall looking for a killer who shot a sheriff back in Missouri. He came to the courthouse jail almost every day and took a look at the new arrivals. The name of the man he was looking for was Joseph P. Dalton.

I guess this sheriff shot and killed a young Indian girl who was off the reservation and running away from him. Dalton shot the sheriff twice in the head and left town. The U.S. Marshall thought Dalton was innocent.

Are you Joseph P. Dalton?"

Yes I am and it feels good to say it. When did you know who I was?" Dalton asked.

"When we first met at the boarding house."

"You did!?"

"Yes. You matched the description and when you put money on the table to help Indians, I knew right away" Landsdown stated.

"You did the right thing by leaving Missouri. If you testified that you killed the sheriff because he shot a young Indian girl, it would have been the same thing as saying you killed the sheriff because he shot a gopher. They would have hanged you!"

"So what is your next stop? The Police?"

"No. I am a lawyer and not an informer. Besides, the deals we made implicate us both. I look forward to doing more business with you Chief Dalton."

"Did you get the Chinese straightened out?"

"Yes. Delightful people but very tight lipped."

"They have to get to know you" Dalton stated.

"It is almost noon! Good grief! I almost forgot your draft! I made it out to Joseph Dillon so you could get the cash before you left. I will leave the ten suitcases at the Trading Post."

"A few days ago, I met a man who thought friendship was better than money. What do you think about that John?"

"I will have to get back to you on that." Landsdown answered.

Dalton nodded and Landsdown left the suite.

When Vincent and Sarah arrived, Dalton put the two suitcases full of money in the buggy and went across the street to cash the draft. When he returned to the buggy, Vincent asked how much Landsdown gave him.

"Just like you said. One thousand twenty-two dollars and seventy-five cents."

Vincent and Sarah walked with Dalton to the station and watched the luggage while he went for his ticket.

When Dalton returned, he gave Sarah a hug and told Vincent to take good care of Piapot's money.

"I have it right here in these saddle bags" Vincent said.

Dalton picked up his luggage and boarded the one o'clock to Lethbridge.

Raincloud and two riders were waiting on the planks as Dalton stepped down from the train. Two riders carried the luggage as they climbed into the buggy and headed for the Gordon Strong Ranch.

"How did everything go?" Raincloud asked.

"Perfect!" Dalton exclaimed.

"Well, Gordon has a large keg on the veranda and the girls are baking soft biscuits" one of the riders said.

"A few mugs and fresh biscuits before supper sounds good to me!" Dalton shouted.

When they reached the ranch, they joined Gordon on the veranda and filled up their mugs.

It sure is nice to clean up our Calgary business" Dalton stated.

"And we have put through another two hundred head of cattle since you left" Gordon continued. "Six days from now, we will bring the money to the village and soak in the hot pool."

The conversation got around to Landsdown and Dalton told them what he knew. They were surprised but not worried. Gordon agreed that Landsdown was very involved in all the dealings and would be the last person to inform.

Dalton told them about the glorified concentration camps and they raised their mugs to Landsdown.

"He is right about the reserves. We are lucky Chief Piapot sent us to the mountains. Every person we put on the plains has money and they know their numbers and letters" Raincloud stated.

After supper, the men went back out to the veranda for more wine.

Early in the morning, the four riders left for the village with Saddle bags full of money. They arrived before noon and left the money in the warriors' room and locked the door.

The dining room was full and everyone was eating lemon pie.

"They are eating our lemon pies as fast as we can bake them!" Beth continued, "Too bad you told them they could eat for free. The nation could make a fortune!"

"What about the deep fried chicken and fish?" Dalton asked.

"That too!" Beth shouted.

Dalton told Beth and Wandering Buffalo about Landsdown. She especially liked what Landsdown had to say about the reserves.

"What about my granddaughter?" Beth asked.

"Sarah is just fine. She has over four thousand dollars in the bank and says she will put in more."

"God! Four thousand dollars! Did you ever guess?!"

"Kinda. I stayed at a fine boarding house in Calgary a few times and Landsdown told her it was for sale. I think she is going to buy it" Dalton said.

"What will that cost?"

"Just a few hundred dollars."

"What about Big Man? Did you get a chance to see him?"

"No. Sarah and Vincent did though. Maybe I should not tell you this but according to them, Big Man appears to be quite happy with his new wife."

"Wife? Three Killer's granddaughter?"

"Yes. They got married in Calgary shortly after he left the village."

"I have nothing against Big Man. I just hope he sticks to one woman!" Beth exclaimed.

"They are moving to Winnipeg. Vincent told him about a place where experience counted. He will be able to take a short cut and learn the white man's medicine. I gave Vincent one hundred dollars for Big Man. Vincent said his family would help out if Big Man continued to learn."

"Good! Do you remember telling us how we would prosper after the money was divided?" Wandering Buffalo asked.

"Yes."

"We spoke with those who were concerned and the assistants made a chart which outlines just about what you said. We will need your approval to post it in the Great Hall" Wandering Buffalo stated.

Dalton nodded and Beth showed him the chart. "Well, what do you think Chief Dalton?" Beth asked.

"The chart is fine but you must add something before I approve it."

"What would you like added?" Beth asked.

"Under the heading 'Village Duties' add this as Item 6.

Chief Elizabeth Buffalo, Chief of Finance, and her assistants, will receive two dollars a day for taking care of village business."

Beth gave Dalton a hug as Wandering Buffalo stood back and smiled.

After putting fifty cents on the small counter, Dalton poured two mugs of wine and left to join Raincloud in the pool.

THE END

Epilogue

Just before nightfall, on September sixth, eighteen hundred and eighty-nine, Michael and Anne rode up to a shack near the railroad just west of Cut Bank. Panes of glass were missing and the door hung on one hinge. Two children were playing on what was left of the veranda.

"Is your father home?" Michael asked.

The children did not answer and went inside. A few minutes later, the father and mother stepped out on the veranda. They looked to be in their early thirties. The father wore patched pants and the mother had several tears in her dress. The father looked like a man who was being worked to death.

"Is your name Wilson?" Michael asked.

"Yes it is and if you came here to collect money for McAllister, you can leave right now!" the father said.

"As a matter of fact, Mr. McAllister left for the east and it would appear as though he had a change of heart. Before leaving, he asked me to give you this envelope."

Michael handed Wilson the envelope and they rode northeast.

"Who are you folks?"

Michael and Anne kept riding until they disappeared over a hill and then turned west to their ranch.

The Wilsons went inside and opened the envelope.

"Three hundred and eighty dollars!!" the father shouted.

"Oh my God!" his wife exclaimed.

They both cried as they picked their children up and held them close.

The Wilsons walked out on the veranda and put the children down to play.

"There was no change of heart. McCallister fooled around with the wrong kind of people."

When they reached the village, Micheal and Anne reported to Dalton.

"Did you give the money to the Wilsons?"

"Yes." Micheal replied.

"What about the flatheads? Did they help you?"

"Yes. There were thirty two head of horses and forty six head of cattle. They wanted the horses and gave us the cattle."

"And I gave the six flatheads ten dollars each." Anne added.

"The village has wedding gifts for you."

The grandparents and Beth brought two children forward.

"This is Angela Louise, a gift for the bride. She is nine years old." Beth continued "And this is Jonathan, a gift for the groom. He is six years old. We have their adoption papers ready for signing if you like the gifts."

"Oh my God! yes!" Anne shouted.

Anne looked at Micheal and he nodded his head.

"Does Jonathan have a second name?" Micheal asked.

"Yes. His second name is Moose." Dalton replied.

There was much laughter as Micheal put moose on his shoulders and left for the church to sign the adoption papers.

The second week in September, the church and cottage were ready for use and the council was called for a final inspection.

"It took a little longer than you thought" Raincloud said.

"Yes. I am learning that some people change their mind in the middle of a job and want a little more" Benjamin said with a smile.

Beth looked the other way as everyone had a good laugh.

The extra work included a twelve-foot addition to the back and a twelve-foot addition to the front. The entrance door was placed in the center and latrines on both sides of the twelve-foot hallway leading to the inside entrance. There was a fireplace in each room.

Behind the raised pulpit and to the right was a hallway leading to a twelve by twelve change room and office for private discussions. There was a small fireplace on the south wall.

To the left of the pulpit was a storage room for cleaning products, wood and coal. The storage room had a hidden hot water line and a cold line. The church could now hold over one hundred people.

The cottage was beautiful. It had two baths, three bedrooms and a very large fireplace in the middle of the east wall. The kitchen and living room was one open room with a huge dining room table in the center. A hidden hot water line and a cold line were installed in the bathrooms and kitchen.

The inside walls were left with a brick and stone finish. The kitchen and doors had a cedar finish. Beams stretched across the ceiling and several lanterns hung from each beam.

When the inspection was over, everyone spoke at once as they praised Benjamin and his builders.

"So I guess you will be heading back to Winnipeg" Beth said.

"No. One of the riders sent a telegram. The kids and Esther will join me in Calgary" Benjamin stated.

"What have you got planned in Calgary?" Raincloud asked.

"Sarah bought a boarding house that needs fixing. We will leave in the morning."

"Well, you and the builders had better come to the top for a soak and a special supper."

"Lemon pie for dessert?" one of the builders asked.

"As much as you can eat!" Wandering Buffalo shouted.

Back in Calgary, Sarah signed the papers for two very new houses.

"How the hell did you come by these two houses for five hundred and sixty dollars? There is even furniture in them" Sarah exclaimed.

"Well, I have a working agreement with the bank whereby they call me first about foreclosures. All they want is their money. These two purchases are not really for me" Landsdown said.

"Too small?"

"Yes. You are very perceptive. All I want from these transactions is the normal legal fee. How are your plans proceeding for the boarding house."

"Very good! Benjamin and his builders will be in Calgary soon to take care of the plumbing and renovations. One of these houses will be for Benjamin and the other one for his builders. Is there such a thing as rent to own?" Sarah asked.

"Of course!"

"Benjamin is a good man. I want a year of his rent to go towards a purchase. If he stays, I will help him get a mortgage for what is owing. If he leaves Calgary, then I will give him some of the rent money he paid and keep the house."

"I can handle that for you. Remember the people who owned these two houses were business men with crazy ideas. A man with too many ideas is sometimes worse off than a man with too few."

"I know. I have been here long enough to see big spenders leave town with just the clothes on their back" Sarah stated.

"Let's get a drink!" Landsdown shouted.

In the warriors' room, Beth and her assistants just finished going over McAllister's documents and Theresa Lone Wolfe gave a report to the council.

"This McAllister did not like paperwork. There are titles here to five ranches. The ranch land and the big house where McAllister lived are still in both their names. He has paperwork which indicated that he gave her five thousand dollars as a complete settlement for the ranch and everything he owns. Take away this paperwork and his wife will get it all.

His marriage papers are here and there are no other papers which point to a divorce or any kind of separation.

There is even his signature on an old Will that leaves his entire estate to his wife.

The daughter still has the east ranch in her name.

Now the other three ranches are foreclosures and he has clear title. His wife is entitled to these three ranches as well" Theresa stated.

"What about bank accounts and a development company owned by him and a fella called Jed?" Dalton asked.

"It is all here. He has bank accounts in Havre and Benton. The total of both these accounts is thirteen thousand, six hundred and eighty dollars plus some interest" Theresa stated.

"I wonder why he had these accounts" Dalton mused.

"Probably so the locals would think he was a man of wealth" Beth offered.

"Now what about this development company?" Dalton asked.

"There is very little money in the account and it just looks like trouble. It should be left alone" Theresa stated.

"You are absolutely right!" Beth agreed.

Everyone nodded.

"Burn the five thousand dollar settlement paperwork and send everything else to his daughter. She will sort it out with her mother. Do you know how to get hold of her?" Dalton asked.

"Yes, it is right here on a letter" Theresa replied.

"McAllister is scattered all over half of Montana. How are they going to prove he is dead?" Beth asked.

"Vincent kinda asked Landsdown that same question. Now according to Landsdown, if an effort is made to contact McAllister and he is not located, he can be deemed legally dead" Dalton replied.

"Deemed?" Raincloud asked.

"I do not know what it means. I think it means you can say he is dead and get your money."

Everyone laughed.

Heather Bright Star, now Heather Star, spoke to the council.

"We have a stack of paper with his personal stamp and nothing else. Why not send her a letter from her father as part of the package? It will not have his signature but somehow we can point out her rights and it will have weight in case she needs something."

"Good idea, I am going to spend money at the bar and we will return at one o'clock to have Heather read us the letter."

Beth and the assistants remained while everyone else went to spend money.

At one o'clock, Heather read the letter.

September 10, 1889.

Dearest Daughter,

I am sorry for everything I have done.

I drove both you and your mother from our home so I could live as a single man. I know I am alone and I will soon end my life. I have had the settlement destroyed.

Everything you and your mother need is in this package.

I know you do not want to see me so speak to your lawyer and proceed to have me deemed legally dead.

Please forgive me,

Your Father.

The package was sent from Benton September 21, 1889.

The first week in October, Sarah entered the great hall and handed Dalton a large sealed envelope. Dalton read the enclosed letter and lowered his head. His long hair covered his face for Dalton was not a man of tears. He handed the letter to Sarah.

Sarah read the letter in a loud voice for all to hear.

Dear Mr. Dalton:

With discretion, I have taken the liberty of having my Winnipeg associate confirm your legal status in the Missouri territory. You will be pleased to know that the circuit judge ordered the last living witness to testify at a trial in your absence.

Under cross examination, the witness testified that after killing the young indian girl, the sheriff turned his gun on you.

The circuit judge offered a scathing assessment of the sheriff and acquitted you.

Enclosed are change of name documents for your entire family. If you so desire, Sarah will bring the signed documents to my office and I will deal with this matter expeditiously.

There will be no charge for these services. Friendship is better than money!

John Landsdown

End of Epilogue